Whispers *in the* Dark

Uncovering Truths Bound by Blood and Betrayal

Rose Jackson-Beavers

Florissant, Mo 63034
Copyright 2024 by Rose Jackson-Beavers

All Rights reserved. No part of this book may be reproduced or transmitted in any forms by any means, electronic, mechanical, photocopy, recording or otherwise, without the consent of the Publisher, except as provided by USA copyright law.

This book is a work of fiction. The incidents, characters, and dialogue are products of the author's imagination and are not to be interpreted as real. Any resemblance to actual people, living or dead, is entirely coincidental.

Edited by Sheliawritesbooks
Cover Designed by Jbookdesigns
Manufactured in the United States of America
Library of Congress Control Number: 2024951278
ISBN: 9798991946407
For information regarding discounts for bulk purchases, please contact Prioritybooks Publications at 1-314-306-2972 or email at beavers_rose@yahoo.com.

Dedication

To my mom, Connie Mae Booker: you are my world. Your tender love and care have been the foundation of my life, and I am endlessly grateful. And to my dad, thank you for always making me feel like I could achieve anything—I will forever carry both your spirits with me.

To my husband, Cedric, my rock and my inspiration, thank you for your unwavering love and for pushing me to reach my highest potential. I thank God for you and for the care you show our family—always steady, always faithful.

To my daughter, Adeesha: you have been by my side in countless ways, acting as my GPS, secretary, shopper, accountant, and partner at events. I am so grateful for you. And to my grandson, Isaiah: remember to dream big! Just as my family has lifted me up, we are here to help you reach your goals. May God bless you always.

To my nieces and nephews, thank you for your unwavering support.

To my siblings and friends: your love inspired me to keep writing. Thank you for always believing in me.

To my readers who have supported me through twenty years of storytelling, thank you from the bottom of my heart. Your loyalty has been a true blessing. And to my sorority, Delta Sigma Theta, thank you for the strength of your sisterhood and your unwavering support!

Dedication

To my mom, Connie Mae Booker: you are my world. Your tender love and care have been the foundation of my life, and I am endlessly grateful. And to my dad, thank you for always making me feel like I could achieve anything—I will forever carry both your spirits with me.

To my husband, Cedric, my rock and my inspiration, thank you for your unwavering love and for pushing me to reach my highest potential. I thank God for you and for the care you show our family—always steady, always faithful.

To my daughter, Adeesha: you have been by my side in countless ways, acting as my GPS, secretary, shopper, accountant, and partner at events. I am so grateful for you. And to my grandson, Isaiah: remember to dream big! Just as my family has lifted me up, we are here to help you reach your goals. May God bless you always.

To my nieces and nephews, thank you for your unwavering support.

To my siblings and friends: your love inspired me to keep writing. Thank you for always believing in me.

To my readers who have supported me through twenty years of storytelling, thank you from the bottom of my heart. Your loyalty has been a true blessing. And to my sorority, Delta Sigma Theta, thank you for the strength of your sisterhood and your unwavering support!

Acknowledgments

To my family, friends, and loyal readers—thank you for joining me on my first adventure into the mystery genre. Writing this novella has been a thrill, though my next project will bring me back to my roots in Christian Romance. Who knows, maybe another mystery awaits in the future! I hope you'll also check out my other books. Your support means everything to me!

<u>Please post reviews at your favorite review site</u>
For more information about me, visit my website
www.rosejacksonbeavers.com

Prelude

Lynette tapped her fingers on the steering wheel. Her speaker rattled out the ringing from her phone. She kept looking from the red light to her cell phone, waiting for Charles to answer.

This was her third time calling his phone. She asked him to stay by the phone in case she needed him, and here he was, being the idiot she knew he could be instead of who she needed at this moment.

"I swear to God if this voicemail comes back on," Lynette began yelling at the steering wheel. The light turned green, and she eased off the brake.

"Come on, dude." Some drool fell from her mouth onto her dark green shirt. "Oh, my God." Disgusted by herself and the situation, she tried to wipe it off, but it was too late. The spit created a wet spot that chilled her, thanks to the autumn night.

"Uh, hello?" His baritone voice invaded her speaker.

"Uh, hello?" Lynette mocked him. Seconds ago, all she wanted was for him to answer. Now that he was on the phone, her desperation was replaced with rage. "I asked you to keep your phone on you. I've called you three times. Are you serious?" Yes, she needed him to guide her, but at this moment, she was putting this necessity on hold as she told him off.

Lynette continued to drive, turning down streets she'd already been down, hoping to return to the point of her journey before she became lost. "Like, simple instructions. I gave you one job, idiot. One darn job, and you couldn't even do that right."

Lynette stopped at another red light. Glancing out the window, she looked to find the name of the street she was on.

If not answering her phone calls when she needed him angered her, his silence, now that he was on the phone, enraged her. "Say something, idiot!

"Damn!"

A soft exhale crackled through the speaker. "I'm just waiting for you to be done, that's all."

"And I was waiting on you to answer your darn phone, but that didn't happen." Lynette was tempted to hang up, but his input was more valuable than gold at this moment.

"I'm on the phone now. Where are you?"

A wave of gratefulness replaced her prior feelings of resentment.

"I'm on Trevor Road. I just passed a gas station."

"Alright," Charles said. He had finally vanquished the dragon that was Lynette's fury. "Was it on your left or right?"

Lynette raised both hands from the steering wheel and extended her pointer finger and thumb to check which one made the letter l, signifying her left side. "My left, it was on my left."

"Woman, you're going the wrong way."

Before Lynette started on another tirade, Charles spoke up. "You're close, though. It should be a movie theater parking lot near you. Turn around on the lot and head back toward the gas station. Two blocks after that, you'll make a right. It's next to a plaza of restaurants."

Lynette looked at the illuminated clock on her dashboard: 1:59 a.m. Instantly, she felt as if a blanket of fatigue had been draped over her. "I don't understand why we couldn't have done this an hour earlier," she uttered while turning into the dark, deserted parking lot.

Lynette pulled up to a grove of bushes that covered the name of the movie theater. Swift movement happened from her side.

"Get out of the damn car!" The voice, so authoritative, so menacing, so out of the blue, caused her to look at who was yelling at who because the person couldn't be yelling at her.

Before Lynette had the chance to press on her accelerator, the butt of a gun crashed into the driver's side window, smashing the glass.

"What the hell was that?" The panic in Charles' voice was palpable, but before Lynette answered, a hand reached in and, in one swift movement, unlocked the door from the inside and yanked it open.

"What—" Before Lynette could say anymore, she was being dragged from her car. She automatically grabbed the steering wheel. Maybe she could put up a big enough fight for the attacker to give up and find an easier target.

"Out of the car!" The person ordered.

Lynette closed her eyes and gripped the steering wheel tighter. Under no circumstances was she going to let him have her car. *Not now, please not now*, Lynette pleaded in her mind.

The butt of the gun smashed against her forehead, causing her self-protection instincts to overpower her need to keep her car.

Lynette let go of the steering wheel, and her body hit the cold pavement. She didn't feel a thing, but adrenaline caused her to grab her injured head, pull herself up, and run for safety.

Go, just go, she yelled internally, struggling to cross the street and go toward the closed restaurants. Maybe a straggler would be around who would help.

The sound of her heart pounding invaded her ears. Running as fast as her legs would take her, Lynette ignored the blood that dripped down her forehead and into her eyes. Her beating heart was replaced by the sound of squealing tires. She stopped and turned to eyeball a person in the driver's seat of her car wearing a Halloween mask. Whoever it was looked at Lynette before speeding off.

At that moment, pain hit her with such force it made her drop to her knees. Her vision doubled, and she went from hot to cold. She cried out but failed to detect anyone around to help her. That's what her fate was going to be for letting go of that steering wheel.

"Woman, you're going the wrong way."

Before Lynette started on another tirade, Charles spoke up. "You're close, though. It should be a movie theater parking lot near you. Turn around on the lot and head back toward the gas station. Two blocks after that, you'll make a right. It's next to a plaza of restaurants."

Lynette looked at the illuminated clock on her dashboard: 1:59 a.m. Instantly, she felt as if a blanket of fatigue had been draped over her. "I don't understand why we couldn't have done this an hour earlier," she uttered while turning into the dark, deserted parking lot.

Lynette pulled up to a grove of bushes that covered the name of the movie theater. Swift movement happened from her side.

"Get out of the damn car!" The voice, so authoritative, so menacing, so out of the blue, caused her to look at who was yelling at who because the person couldn't be yelling at her.

Before Lynette had the chance to press on her accelerator, the butt of a gun crashed into the driver's side window, smashing the glass.

"What the hell was that?" The panic in Charles' voice was palpable, but before Lynette answered, a hand reached in and, in one swift movement, unlocked the door from the inside and yanked it open.

"What—" Before Lynette could say anymore, she was being dragged from her car. She automatically grabbed the steering wheel. Maybe she could put up a big enough fight for the attacker to give up and find an easier target.

"Out of the car!" The person ordered.

Lynette closed her eyes and gripped the steering wheel tighter. Under no circumstances was she going to let him have her car. *Not now, please not now,* Lynette pleaded in her mind.

The butt of the gun smashed against her forehead, causing her self-protection instincts to overpower her need to keep her car.

Lynette let go of the steering wheel, and her body hit the cold pavement. She didn't feel a thing, but adrenaline caused her to grab her injured head, pull herself up, and run for safety.

Go, just go, she yelled internally, struggling to cross the street and go toward the closed restaurants. Maybe a straggler would be around who would help.

The sound of her heart pounding invaded her ears. Running as fast as her legs would take her, Lynette ignored the blood that dripped down her forehead and into her eyes. Her beating heart was replaced by the sound of squealing tires. She stopped and turned to eyeball a person in the driver's seat of her car wearing a Halloween mask. Whoever it was looked at Lynette before speeding off.

At that moment, pain hit her with such force it made her drop to her knees. Her vision doubled, and she went from hot to cold. She cried out but failed to detect anyone around to help her. That's what her fate was going to be for letting go of that steering wheel.

CHAPTER 1

Two Days Later

Gabi stared up at the ceiling of her bedroom. Just a few hours ago, she was in a bar, waiting around to spot him. She kept looking at his picture on the dating app that connected them, worrying that she might have been catfished or he wouldn't be happy with how she looked. Gabi was very conscious of having a flattering picture that was not misleading. However, she did pick one that made her hair look more curly than frizzy, and her stomach looked a lot flatter than it was in the pink skirt and white top she was wearing.

I should have suggested a better lit place, Gabi thought as she looked at each male, waiting to examine identifiable features of the man she matched with. His green eyes, pearly white smile, and silky dark hair were burned in her mind. She kept looking at his picture to make sure she wasn't imagining the Hispanic adonis she was waiting for.

A deep inhale and movement from the other side of the bed drew her eyes to him. Just a few hours ago, they were strangers. Then, within a matter of moments, they were connected through their conversation. It seemed that not knowing each other well allowed them to be freer.

Gabi was looking for a friend. She was an attractive young woman with a good job but didn't want a relationship. Plenty of people were going to the internet to meet and spend a night of fun together without the commitment, and that was exactly what she wanted. She was straddling the fence of sinning and trying to live a life that pleased God. But still, she was lonely. All she needed was someone to talk to and to have a little fun, and a kiss or two would make it all the better. It was hard for single women to find companionship. It was the reason she tried one of those sites where you used an app to meet someone then keep it moving if you didn't hit it off.

Seeking companionship on the internet was embarrassing, but finally, she met him. His name was Lester—that's all she knew or expected to find out. *Let's just keep it simple,* she thought.

Lester, who was looking for the same thing. Neither wanted relationships but wanted to have a connection with the opposite sex, just to talk sometimes. They connected and scheduled a date to meet. She wasn't scared because the site did thorough background checks to ensure the people were legitimate and didn't have criminal backgrounds.

She and Lester went to a hotel restaurant and spent time talking and getting to know each other. It was a fun date with no strings attached. They kept the conversation clean and discussed things like politics, relationships, social media platforms, and other general conversations.

I'm too old for this foolishness, she thought. She wished she were already dating or had a marital relationship, but that wasn't in the cards for her. She just wanted someone to be affectionate with and to have an understanding. She needed to start off as friends because she didn't want to return to her old way of thinking, which was to head to a hotel for a rump in bed. That was old. That was scary and not what a Christian would do. She only scheduled the meeting in a hotel restaurant because it was trendy, and most people went to experience their tasty food.

Seated at the table, the atmosphere between Gabi and Lester was a mixture of anticipation and curiosity. She was attracted to him and hoped he wanted to lay eyes on her again. She raked her hand through her big fluffy afro.

They perused the menu, exchanging glances and occasional smiles.

"So, Gabi," Lester began, "what made you decide to try a platform like this to meet people?"

"I wanted to meet someone and get to know then, you know,

someone I didn't know. Doing something different than I've done before."

Lester nodded in understanding. "I get that. It's hard to find that middle ground these days."

Their conversation flowed, touching on various topics like their careers, hobbies, and some of their favorite childhood memories. Lester was a chemical engineer with a passion for photography, and Gabi was immersed in the world of writing. They discovered common ground in their love for travel and a shared distaste for pineapple on pizza.

The waiter approached and took their orders. As they delved deeper into personal stories, the initial awkwardness dissipated, replaced by a genuine connection.

"Do you have any siblings, Gabi?"

Gabi smiled. "Yeah, I have a younger brother. He's a handful, but I wouldn't trade him for the world. How about you?"

Lester chuckled. "I'm the baby of the family. Two older sisters who made sure I grew up with a healthy appreciation for '80s rock music."

As they continued to share stories, the conversation shifted to their views on relationships. Gabi couldn't help but address the elephant in the room. "So, Lester, what are you really looking for on this platform? No judgments, just curious."

Lester met her gaze, his expression thoughtful. "Honestly, Gabi, I'm looking for a connection. Someone to talk to, share moments with, without the pressure of a traditional relationship. I've been there, done that. Now, I just want simplicity and authenticity. How about you?"

Gabi appreciated his honesty. "Same here. I want to enjoy someone's company without the complications. Life is complicated enough, right?"

Their orders arrived, and they continued their discussion, savoring the food and the newfound connection that seemed to be growing stronger with every shared moment.

An hour and forty-five minutes later, Gabi stood up, signaling the end of their evening. Lester, appreciating her company, rose from his seat and suggested walking her to her car.

"It's not necessary to walk me to the car. You stay and enjoy your food. I have to make it home. I have a huge meeting in the morning," Gabi said, attempting to keep things casual.

Lester smiled and replied, "I don't mind. It's a gentlemanly thing to do, right?"

Gabi chuckled. "Well, I appreciate the gentlemanly gesture, but it's really not required. Besides, we've just met."

Lester insisted. "I'd feel better making sure you return to your car safely. Humor me, Gabi."

With a playful roll of her eyes, Gabi agreed. "Alright, you can walk me to my car, but no need to wait until I drive away. I'm a big girl; I can handle myself."

As they walked through the hotel lobby, the atmosphere was

a mix of comfort and uncertainty. They engaged in light banter about the evening, discussing their favorite parts of the conversation. Lester steered away from any romantic undertones, keeping the mood friendly and relaxed.

Reaching the parking lot, they stopped by Gabi's car. She turned to him and said, "Thanks for the company, Lester. It was a pleasant surprise."

Lester grinned. "Likewise, Gabi. I enjoyed our talk. Maybe we can do it again sometime."

"Sure, maybe," Gabi replied, her tone suggesting a hint of reservation.

Lester extended his hand for a handshake, but before Gabi extended her hand, he pulled her into a warm hug. Caught off guard, she hesitated for a moment before relaxing into the embrace. Lester released her, offering a friendly smile.

"Take care, Gabi. Until next time."

Gabi, somewhat flustered, replied, "You too, Lester."

As she drove away, Gabi replayed the evening in her mind, contemplating her unexpected connection and the uncertain path ahead.

Elyse was standing at the Plexiglas door, looking out, waiting. The sun shone through the glass, creating a prism that fell just short of her black kitten heels.

moments with, without the pressure of a traditional relationship. I've been there, done that. Now, I just want simplicity and authenticity. How about you?"

Gabi appreciated his honesty. "Same here. I want to enjoy someone's company without the complications. Life is complicated enough, right?"

Their orders arrived, and they continued their discussion, savoring the food and the newfound connection that seemed to be growing stronger with every shared moment.

An hour and forty-five minutes later, Gabi stood up, signaling the end of their evening. Lester, appreciating her company, rose from his seat and suggested walking her to her car.

"It's not necessary to walk me to the car. You stay and enjoy your food. I have to make it home. I have a huge meeting in the morning," Gabi said, attempting to keep things casual.

Lester smiled and replied, "I don't mind. It's a gentlemanly thing to do, right?"

Gabi chuckled. "Well, I appreciate the gentlemanly gesture, but it's really not required. Besides, we've just met."

Lester insisted. "I'd feel better making sure you return to your car safely. Humor me, Gabi."

With a playful roll of her eyes, Gabi agreed. "Alright, you can walk me to my car, but no need to wait until I drive away. I'm a big girl; I can handle myself."

As they walked through the hotel lobby, the atmosphere was

a mix of comfort and uncertainty. They engaged in light banter about the evening, discussing their favorite parts of the conversation. Lester steered away from any romantic undertones, keeping the mood friendly and relaxed.

Reaching the parking lot, they stopped by Gabi's car. She turned to him and said, "Thanks for the company, Lester. It was a pleasant surprise."

Lester grinned. "Likewise, Gabi. I enjoyed our talk. Maybe we can do it again sometime."

"Sure, maybe," Gabi replied, her tone suggesting a hint of reservation.

Lester extended his hand for a handshake, but before Gabi extended her hand, he pulled her into a warm hug. Caught off guard, she hesitated for a moment before relaxing into the embrace. Lester released her, offering a friendly smile.

"Take care, Gabi. Until next time.

Gabi, somewhat flustered, replied, "You too, Lester."

As she drove away, Gabi replayed the evening in her mind, contemplating her unexpected connection and the uncertain path ahead.

Elyse was standing at the Plexiglas door, looking out, waiting. The sun shone through the glass, creating a prism that fell just short of her black kitten heels.

"Where is he?" She removed her glasses and began cleaning them on her burgundy turtleneck that matched her leather skirt. As she put her spectacles back on her face, Elyse sighed and looked out toward the street. Her hands went to her hair, making sure that her gray flyaway was going to her bun.

She reached in her purse and pulled out her cell phone. The clock on her phone showed 9:47 am. As she swiped to go to her wallpaper, she caught her reflection on the black screen. Her eyes and mouth were surrounded by lines that told a story of a long life. Each crease in her dark brown skin was a testament to being in the world for 65 years.

Elyse opened her local news app. Her screen turned a bright blue as the words THE BRIDGETON BUGLE, in large white letters, filled her screen before it vanished and brought up a selection of local news stories to click on. Elyse's eyes scanned the page and clicked on the first link that led her to: "Authorities Still Searching for Missing Carjacking Victim."

A picture of a smiling Lynette beamed from Elyse's screen as her eyes began to skim the article. The words "blood puddle on Trevor Road, 2:00 a.m., eyewitnesses and suspects jumped out at Elyse as she scrolled through the article.

A series of three short knocks broke her concentration and scared her. She rapidly looked up to glaze at Lester. His bright eyes seemed to shine brighter due to his brown Latino skin. He wore gray slacks, a black button-up shirt, and a yellow tie.

He caught the door when Elyse opened it, smiled at her sheepishly, and walked in.

"I'm sorry. I thought I'd be able to park on the lot." His teeth looked like a string of straight ivory as he smiled at Elyse before looking around the foyer.

A security guard sat at the desk, watching them with a clipboard in front of him for visitors to sign before gaining entrance into the building. A glass sign on the front of the desk read: "Oriflamme Productions: The Rallying Call for the Learned."

"Not until you secure your badge. Then you'll be able to use the parking lot and have access to the building on your own." Elyse's voice was firm and held the irritation she experienced due to his tardiness. She looked down at her phone. It said 9:49 a.m. He was supposed to be here at nine forty-five. *If this is how he's going to be on his first day, he might have to leave now.* She led him into the building and toward the offices.

"Reading anything fun?" Lester's voice invaded Elyse's thoughts.

Elyse turned her head, looked at him, and depicted a look of desperation to be back in her good graces, and her heart softened. She stopped and used her thumb to scroll to the top of the article. Once she arrived at the spot, she held the phone up to show him what she was reading. "Not fun, just sad. Can you believe this?"

Lester's eyes narrowed as he leaned forward and began to scan the introductory paragraph. The interior lights from the facility lit up his attractive features. His silky but somewhat coarse hair caught the shine of the light and almost blinded Elyse. His eyes were focused, and he seemed to be soaking in as much information as he could. He rose to a normal standing position and furrowed his brow. "When did this happen?"

Elyse looked back at her screen and scrolled through the article. "Uhh…three days ago, well, nights," she corrected herself. She locked her phone and put it back into her purse before turning back to show him around his new work environment and office.

"That's too bad." He looked around as if trying to find a new topic to change to while soaking in his new surroundings.

Lester smiled and nodded, looking in awe at the studio. "I never miss it. Helped my credit score increase to 800 plus."

Elyse stopped and smiled at him, admiring him for his responsibility. "That's great. I figured you weren't one of those people who just make stupid mistakes. I like that about you."

Lester smiled and said, "I like how you want people to be better than their situations. You guys do a lot of neighborhood outreach. That's why I wanted to work at this station."

Elyse smiled and started leading him through the multiple studios. As they walked past the trophy holder that held multiple relics of the studio's excellence in programming, Lester began to take everything in. Other people milled around, some looking busy, some looking worried, and others looking bored.

The sound of phones ringing in the background became white noise to Lester as he followed Elyse.

As they walked, he became aware of her before she did him. Her eyes were buried in her phone's screen. As they were about to pass each other, she looked up. When her eyes caught his, Gabi stopped in midstride. Embarrassment, surprise, and confusion covered her face in a matter of milliseconds.

"Hi," she uttered, trying to play it cool.

"Nice to meet you." He nodded at her, making sure she understood that he wasn't going to let their date be known to anyone.

"This is you." Elyse's stern voice broke through Gabi and Lester's awkwardness.

Lester could feel the daggers Elyse was throwing at Gabi as she walked away. She used her arm to usher him into the room.

Lester confidently walked into the room, taking it all in. His desk faced the door, and he had a window behind him. The walls were blank, except for a calendar that had upcoming events on it.

"If you need me," Elyse said, interrupting his thoughts, "I'm two doors down." Elyse shut the door and walked away. Though the hallway was littered with noise, Lester listened to her small heels hitting the floor with each determined step she made.

CHAPTER 2

Lester's once-empty office was now cluttered with small stacks of paperwork on his desk and windowsill. A gentle knock on his door interrupted his focus on the computer screen. "Come in."

Gabi entered, her full stature not fully appreciated during their earlier conversation at the restaurant. Standing at no more than 5'4", she asked, "Do you mind if I come in?"

"Nah, go ahead." Lester gestured to the empty chair opposite his desk. Gabi shut the door and settled into the seat.

"What's your name again?" She smiled, a hint of embarrassment playing on her features. She played coy, her brown skin complemented by the bright blue dress with white trim. Her large hoops seamlessly blended with her coarse, black, fluffy curls.

"Lester. What's yours?" He tried to discern from her name badge, but she twisted it in her hands. Both were cautious, believing they had exchanged fake names.

"Gabi." She rose, offering her hand to shake.

Lester shook it, noting her unconventional gesture. She had done the same at the hotel restaurant, which struck him as odd. When was the last time a woman offered to shake his hand during an introduction?

"So, what do you do here?" Gabi leaned back, getting comfortable.

"I'm the PR manager, monitoring ads and getting new advertisers. You?"

"I work in the legal department, reviewing contracts for errors before they're sent out for signatures."

"Okay." Lester nodded. "Do you like working here?" he asked, leaning back.

"It's all right. The only annoying thing is Elyse." Gabi imitated Elyse's strict demeanor, "I do not like loafers. If you don't want to work, then you can leave now! Give it a rest, lady. Like she has any room to talk."

"What do you mean?" Lester leaned forward in interest.

Gabi shook her head, rolling her eyes. "She truly does nothing here. Like, if her son wasn't who he was, she would—"

A loud knock at the door interrupted them. The door swung open, revealing Elyse. She stepped into the room, stood next to Gabi, and looked down at her.

Gabi seemed disinterested, ignoring Elyse's presence. She maintained a poker face, refusing to show any reaction to Elyse's insinuations.

"I'm glad you've met Gabi. She likes to make herself known to the men in the building." Elyse said, shooting a condescending smile at Gabi.

Gabi's facial expression remained stoic, resembling the Zen of a Buddhist monk striving for nirvana. She kept a poker face while Elyse was next to her. If she was bothered by Elyse's insinuations, she refused to show it.

"Yeah." Lester smiled awkwardly. "Gabi's been nice to me, just like she is to everyone in the building, especially the women." Lester looked at Gabi to discern if she recognized how he tried to deflect attention from her, but Gabi's eyes did not waver.

"I need the approval of those forms when you have a chance," Elyse said, her thick African accent carrying authority. Before Lester responded, Elyse pivoted on her heels and stormed away.

Gabi smiled as if reading Lester's mind. "All right, I just wanted to come and formally meet you and inform you that a few of us are going to happy hour at the Burger Barn across the street after work. Please join us."

"Okay," Lester said and turned back to his computer screen.

"A man of few words." Gabi laughed. "Ok, catch you later." She closed the door behind her before walking away.

Once Gabi's footsteps got further from his office, Lester opened a new window in his internet server. The Oriflamme home page popped up. He went to the company's directory and opened it. In the search box, he typed in "Gabrielle." Five results popped up. He clicked on the only Gabrielle who worked in Legal, and her work information filled the screen: Gabrielle Munn, Legal Analyst, Extension 5690, followed by her date of employment and some other information.

Lester's eyes absorbed the information and nodded. "Okay, Gabi. I'll catch you tonight."

The wooded area bordering the Ravenwood Lakes neighborhood served as the favored spot for the weekly Friday night bonfire hosted by Bridgeton High School teenagers. Among the mix of colorful hair and clothes proudly donned by the attendees were several kids sporting the school's colors, blue and gold.

"I'm not sure if I wanna be out here tonight," sixteen-year-old Hannah complained, surveying the other teens. "It's a musty scent out here." Holding their noses, Hannah frowned. "What is that stench? It's awful." She pulled her hair tie from her ponytail, restyling her hair into a bun. Her silky brunette hair, coupled with the setting horizon, cast a slight aura on her ivory skin.

A few teens nodded and murmured in agreement with Hannah's remarks until Deante, an eighteen-year-old Black alpha male, stepped forward. "Nah, y'all." His strong voice seemed to reverberate through the trees. "Isn't this tradition? And once the fire is started, we won't be able to inhale that stench, whatever it is anyway."

Lisa rolled her eyes and leaned toward George, whispering, "Who put him in charge? Isn't this his first time here?"

Some teenagers cast their eyes to the ground, almost ashamed they were considering leaving during Deante's time of need. He appeared to be back in full spirits after being kicked off the football team a few weeks ago.

Deante always seemed like he had something to prove, as if he had finally found his niche with football. After making the varsity team his freshman year, he was an envied running back. It seemed destined that colleges would scout him. However, an incident at a party led to his removal from the team.

Rumors spread, but Deante never addressed or denied them. He started to keep to himself afterward. Now that Deante was ready to move back into the swing of high school society, no one wanted to impede his re-emergence.

Lisa sighed. "Let's light the fire pit."

George reached next to the pit, grabbed the bottle of lighter fluid, and began pouring it on the wood.

Deante smiled. "I'll go get more wood so the fire can last long."

"Cool," said George as Deante started walking off.

"I'll come with you." Hannah ran to catch up.

"I swear, the thirst. The unadulterated desperation she has for him." Lisa pulled a lighter out of her pocket and activated the flame. "We have enough wood," she muttered, placing the flickering fire onto the heap.

Lisa believed she should have been happy for her friend, Hannah, for breaking out of her shy shell, but she couldn't understand why Hannah seemed to crave Deante's approval so much.

Some people probably thought Lisa was jealous that she was losing her best friend to a guy, but that wasn't the case.

Lisa and Hannah had been friends since freshman year in Civics class, where their last names placed them in desks across from each other. Despite being best friends, they were like Ying and Yang, both in personality and appearance. While Hannah was pale, Lisa was a dark-skinned Black girl. Hannah was too trusting and naive, whereas Lisa questioned everything and everyone. So, while everyone else was excited to have Deante join their Friday night tradition, something about his sudden appearance and Hannah's desperation annoyed Lisa.

"I just think he's overrated with his stupid pep-talk. Okay, guys! Let's start the fire. Hut, one-two, one-two," Lisa mocked.

The other kids burst into laughter as Lisa continued her show, trying to set the fire.

Montoya, a short seventeen-year-old, shushed Lisa as the wood caught fire. "Stop complaining." She looked around to make sure Deante wasn't around to hear Lisa, then scrunched her nose at the foul odor. "Oh, my God, it's funky. Stinks like Larry's momma!"

The teens laughed as Larry stepped up, angry. He was about to defend his mother's honor when a sharp yell pierced through the woods. The sound came from the direction that Deante and

Hannah walked in. Before any of the teenagers had the opportunity to process what was going on, the quick and heavy footsteps of the two were coming back toward the fire pit.

"Oh, my God, someone call 911!" Hannah yelled as she ran up to the group with her phone in her hand. Her eyes were covered in fear, and her forehead was saturated with worry. The shock must have made her forget how to work the device in her hand. Instead of calling the police, Hannah used her phone to point in the direction that she and Deante fled from. "In that spot is a lady… she's not moving! I think she's dead."

"What?" Lisa ran in the direction Hannah and Deante ran from, passing Deante as he stood back from the crowd, crying with his hands over his head. As Lisa ran, the stench grew stronger.

"Wait! Come back!" Someone yelled after Lisa.

For some reason, that made Lisa pump her legs faster, wanting to reach the destination before anyone stopped her. With each step, the odor in the air grew thicker and heavier. Lisa ingested the taste of the stench in her mouth as she ran. Three feet in front of her, she witnessed the body of a woman partially covered in leaves.

Lisa imagined what she expected to see, but seeing it was a different story. Her mind took in every detail of the body in a matter of seconds. The way the body's skin was pale and bloated, the way wildlife had made a meal of her fingers, the maggots that wiggled in the gaping hole in her forehead, and the green shirt that seemed almost bright in comparison to the dead foliage that covered her body. The sight burned itself into her memory, and she let out a piercing scream of horror. She expected that she would never be able to unsee those images out of her mind for the rest of her life.

The sound of sirens filled the street as police cars and an ambulance drove past Lester walking into the Burger Barn. With the door closed behind him, the sirens were replaced with music as he scanned the restaurant, searching for Gabi. Once he spotted her, he began approaching the table of six other coworkers.

"I can't believe she's been missing for close to two weeks now, and nothing?" Gabi looked up from the group and spotted Lester standing at the table. "Hey!" She gestured to the whole table. "Everyone, this is Lester. Lester," she began, pointing to each person individually. "This is Autumn, Frank, Xavier, Paul, Amy, and Parris."

Lester smiled at everyone as Gabi grabbed a seat and pulled it up to the table.

"Thanks," he said and sat down. "Who are you guys talking about?"

Gabi handed him the happy hour menu. "We just ordered. You should too so we can receive our food at the same time. They have two-dollar sliders until seven. I suggest those, and they make a great White Russian, but we were talking about Lynette Newble. She was—"

Hannah walked in. Before any of the teenagers had the opportunity to process what was going on, the quick and heavy footsteps of the two were coming back toward the fire pit.

"Oh, my God, someone call 911!" Hannah yelled as she ran up to the group with her phone in her hand. Her eyes were covered in fear, and her forehead was saturated with worry. The shock must have made her forget how to work the device in her hand. Instead of calling the police, Hannah used her phone to point in the direction that she and Deante fled from. "In that spot is a lady… she's not moving! I think she's dead."

"What?" Lisa ran in the direction Hannah and Deante ran from, passing Deante as he stood back from the crowd, crying with his hands over his head. As Lisa ran, the stench grew stronger.

"Wait! Come back!" Someone yelled after Lisa.

For some reason, that made Lisa pump her legs faster, wanting to reach the destination before anyone stopped her. With each step, the odor in the air grew thicker and heavier. Lisa ingested the taste of the stench in her mouth as she ran. Three feet in front of her, she witnessed the body of a woman partially covered in leaves.

Lisa imagined what she expected to see, but seeing it was a different story. Her mind took in every detail of the body in a matter of seconds. The way the body's skin was pale and bloated, the way wildlife had made a meal of her fingers, the maggots that wiggled in the gaping hole in her forehead, and the green shirt that seemed almost bright in comparison to the dead foliage that covered her body. The sight burned itself into her memory, and she let out a piercing scream of horror. She expected that she would never be able to unsee those images out of her mind for the rest of her life.

The sound of sirens filled the street as police cars and an ambulance drove past Lester walking into the Burger Barn. With the door closed behind him, the sirens were replaced with music as he scanned the restaurant, searching for Gabi. Once he spotted her, he began approaching the table of six other coworkers.

"I can't believe she's been missing for close to two weeks now, and nothing?" Gabi looked up from the group and spotted Lester standing at the table. "Hey!" She gestured to the whole table. "Everyone, this is Lester. Lester," she began, pointing to each person individually. "This is Autumn, Frank, Xavier, Paul, Amy, and Parris."

Lester smiled at everyone as Gabi grabbed a seat and pulled it up to the table.

"Thanks," he said and sat down. "Who are you guys talking about?"

Gabi handed him the happy hour menu. "We just ordered. You should too so we can receive our food at the same time. They have two-dollar sliders until seven. I suggest those, and they make a great White Russian, but we were talking about Lynette Newble. She was—"

Lester studied the menu and then began to look for a server. "Yeah, the lady who's missing, right?"

Parris shook her head emphatically. "No one's heard from her. Not her mother, no one."

"They might as well cut that loss," Frank said before sipping his drink. "Better call the insurance company and obtain the money. She's not coming back."

Oh my goodness, Frank," Gabi yelled, "that's someone's daughter!"

"And now it's someone's corpse," Frank smirked.

Xavier and Lester began to laugh as the women looked at them disgusted.

"You're friends with her, Gabi. Where do you think she is?" Xavier asked as the server approached their table.

"A new customer," the server noted, nodding at Lester while reaching into his apron pocket and pulling out a pen. "Are you ready to order?"

"Yes, I'll take five of your pepper jack cheese sliders, macaroni poppers, and—"

"Six or eight poppers?"

"Six, and a lemonade."

"Got it. I'll put that in right now." The server ripped the order off his pad and slipped the pen back into his pocket.

Lester turned back to the group and looked at Gabi. "You and her were friends?"

"We worked together, and I didn't have a relationship with her like that, but we were cool."

"She was annoying," Xavier lambasted.

Autumn buried her head in her hand with annoyance. "I swear to God, we can't take y'all anywhere."

Frank laughed, loving to get a rise out of the girls. "She was, but she was hilarious when she got me."

"Oh, my God, remember when she went off on Elyse?" Parris jumped in.

"Don't encourage them, Parris." Gabi stopped them. "Like I said, we were cool, went running a few times in the park, and we sometimes ate together. I can't believe that she's missing, and they were so quick to fill her office, not knowing if she's going to come back or not."

The server approached the table, gave Lester his lemonade, and then went about refilling the empty water glasses from the pitcher of water he had brought with him.

"Who has her office?" Lester asked, about to take a sip from his drink.

"You," Xavier said nonchalantly.

Lester stopped mid-sip, pooling the lemonade in his mouth, unsure if he should swallow or spit it back in his cup. He had a sneaky suspicion that if he were to swallow at that moment, he would begin to choke, so he waited until the muscles in his throat calmed and settled down to relax his esophagus.

"Don't worry, it's not haunted if that's what you're thinking about," Frank joked.

Lester swallowed and laughed. "Nah, I just wasn't expecting you to say me. I thought you were going to mention that new chick from accounting or something." The table laughed. "How long have all of you been working at Oriflamme?"

"Too long. Is that an okay answer?" Frank asked.

Gabi shook her head, ignoring him. "I've been working for this company for close to six years. Frank's been employed for like a year, and—"

"I've been working for two years," Parris chimed in. "Xavier and Autumn came during the summer."

Lester looked around, studying their faces, as if trying to drink in their words as if they were the refreshment he needed, but his eyes kept admiring Gabi's face.

Gabi's face had a reassurance to it that seemed to exude genuineness. With each unadulterated emotion, her face expressed ease. She was animated, but not to the point of putting on a show, but as a true expression of her reactions, emotions, and thoughts.

Her face was full and youthful. Though she was no younger than 35, she looked like she was in her twenties.

"Do you like working at this company?" Lester looked at their faces.

Frank shrugged his shoulders. "It's a check."

Everyone else at the table nodded in agreement, except for Gabi.

Gabi smiled sheepishly. "I don't know. I mean, it could be worse."

"Especially if you were Lynette," Frank couldn't help himself.

Before Gabi expressed her distaste, the servers came with a large tray and began placing plates of food in front of each of them.

It was a little after ten. The group was putting on their jackets and walking toward the door, with Gabi and Lester trailing behind the others.

"Thanks for coming, Lester." Gabi smiled, then looked down at the buttons on her jacket as she attempted to put them through their corresponding holes.

"We do this every other Friday, so you're welcome to come." Gabi smiled and began to dig in her purse for her keys.

Lester nodded. "All right, I'll make sure I make a note of it." He held the door open for Gabi and allowed her to exit, then followed her out as they walked in the same direction to their cars.

Gabi pulled her phone out of her purse and tapped the home button. At the top were multiple text message notifications. About three feet from her car, she stopped and looked at her phone, mouth agape.

"What?" Lester's concern showed more in his voice than it

did on his face, but when she looked at him, he was caught with a quick look of terror.

Gabi's facial expression revealed a hodgepodge of emotions from panic, fear, anger, and confusion. The myriad of emotions molded on her face with powerful stoicism. The only clear outward expression was the tears that slid from each corner of her eyes. Her mouth was still open as she attempted to use her lips to form the words she prayed she wouldn't have to say: "I think they found Lynette's body."

CHAPTER 3

The tears flowing down her cheeks washed away Hannah's over-the-counter facial foundation. She looked at the homicide detectives across the table from her, her mother cradling Hannah's head against her chest in an attempt to soothe her daughter.

Detective LaFlore asked Hannah, "How did you end up in the woods?"

"Every Friday night, we have a bonfire in the neighborhood. We sit around and talk, roast goodies, and that's about it." Hannah's voice, ravaged by tears, sounded grizzled and hoarse. The crying not only destroyed her makeup but also took its toll on her vocal cords.

Detective Morris looked at his notes and flipped to the page with other names of people who were present. "And the kids there, they're usually always attending.

Yeah, uh—well, no. It was Deante's first time."

did on his face, but when she looked at him, he was caught with a quick look of terror.

Gabi's facial expression revealed a hodgepodge of emotions from panic, fear, anger, and confusion. The myriad of emotions molded on her face with powerful stoicism. The only clear outward expression was the tears that slid from each corner of her eyes. Her mouth was still open as she attempted to use her lips to form the words she prayed she wouldn't have to say: "I think they found Lynette's body."

CHAPTER 3

The tears flowing down her cheeks washed away Hannah's over-the-counter facial foundation. She looked at the homicide detectives across the table from her, her mother cradling Hannah's head against her chest in an attempt to soothe her daughter.

Detective LaFlore asked Hannah, "How did you end up in the woods?"

"Every Friday night, we have a bonfire in the neighborhood. We sit around and talk, roast goodies, and that's about it." Hannah's voice, ravaged by tears, sounded grizzled and hoarse. The crying not only destroyed her makeup but also took its toll on her vocal cords.

Detective Morris looked at his notes and flipped to the page with other names of people who were present. "And the kids there, they're usually always attending.

Yeah, uh—well, no. It was Deante's first time."

"And Deante was with you when you discovered the body, right?"

Hannah nodded and closed her eyes, a horrible mistake as her mind assaulted her with the image of the dead woman's body. Her chin quivered, she shook her head, and fresh tears swelled in her eyes, slipping past her closed eyelids.

The two homicide detectives looked at each other and nodded, signifying the end of the meeting with the fragile teen. Detective Morris slid Hannah's written statement to her. "Could you re-read this, ensure it's correct, then sign it?" He gestured to her mother to do the same, and she nodded.

Hannah's eyes went over the page. Seeing the words "odor," "body," and "dead," she couldn't look at any other words. She scribbled her name on the designated line, dated it, and then slid it to her mother to sign before bursting into tears again. Her mother added her chicken scratch to the paper, dropped the pen, and then cradled her daughter's head to her bosom again. She then guided Hannah to stand up and led her toward the exit. Detectives Morris and LaFlore surveyed Hannah's mother guide her to the door. Every few steps, they caught Hannah sniffling until she finally left. The two homicide detectives looked at each other.

Deante sat in the interrogation room, fidgeting and shaking his legs. On the other side of the door, he listened to Hannah sobbing, shushed by her mother as she left. For a moment, Deante was jealous and wished he'd called his mother, but then immediately became relieved she wasn't there. He couldn't handle her forceful communication style that seemed to so easily offend others. He witnessed how easily a conversation with her could turn from a tête-à-tête to something volatile. Within a fleeting moment, a tear appeared in the corner of his eye as he thought about how much he missed his father.

His father was his rock, his support, and was there to help him through the rough times of his life before he left. Three years ago, his father was his advocate when things got tough with his mother. When his mother would accuse him of things that he didn't do, or things that were normal for a teenager to do, his father would step in and try to diffuse the situation. After his father left, Deante tried to seek solace in his brother but kept coming up empty.

"I don't understand why you care about him," Charles's voice reverberated through the phone. "He didn't care about us enough to stay, so why care about him?"

Tears began to pour even more as Deante remembered the conversation with his brother. "Because you don't realize how it is to be with Mommy. You're gone, but I'm stuck with her, and the only person I expect to always be on my side is gone. Like, why did he leave? He couldn't have waited until I left for college?"

Charles let out a loud, exaggerated sigh. "Look, Mommy's not perfect, but it could be worse."

Deante wanted to hang up on his brother. He hated it when Charles would say stuff like that. He already figured it could have been worse. He didn't need Charles to remind him. He could have been homeless. He could have been like the guy in the movie, "The Blindside." With his father, he believed it was okay to be himself. That no matter what, he was loved. But with his mother, he internalized the pressure to be perfect. Any emotion that wasn't joy was an offense to her. He recognized that he had to be a shell of himself and that no matter what, his mother was looking for one of his flaws to attack him.

Common sense taught him through life that his mother loved him. It was evident from the things that she did. He remembered when he was sick, she would be by his side while he vomited at night. But he always came short with his heart accepting that her love was conditional, and at any time, she might drop him. However, in her eyesight, her beloved Charles, whom she worshipped, could blow up an orphanage, and she would love him regardless.

Living in his mother's house caused such anxiety that he could feel his chest throbbing and his breath becoming labored just thinking about how she affected him. He put his hand on his heart, feeling it move slowly and then faster. He breathed in and out to gain control.

Charles, who was in his 30s and who'd moved out years ago, didn't have the same stress of living with their mother. He hoped that Charles would understand, but he didn't. Deante just wanted a moment to be open to someone and the freedom to express his unhappiness without having to qualify it. He had that with his father, but with him gone, he didn't have that anymore.

Deante's shoulders heaved as he reacted to the realization that he experienced such isolation in his life. The doors opened, and Detectives Morris and LaFlore walked in.

Deante looked up and began to wipe his face. The detectives quietly approached the table and sat down. Detective Morris leaned forward, looking at Deante. "Do you need some time?"

Deante's face was clear from the tears. The only evidence of him crying was the redness of his eyes. "Nah. I'm good."

Detective Morris nodded, sliding a box of tissues toward Deante. "I guess finding a dead body in the woods would be emotional for anyone."

Deante felt like time paused for a second as his mind tried to grapple with the sentence Detective Morris had just said. At that moment, everything hit him, and he remembered why he was there. He grabbed a tissue and began to cover his face as he heaved again. He couldn't stop the tears. He wiped his face with the tissue and closed his eyes. He shook his head and looked at the detectives.

Detectives LaFlore and Detective Morris exchanged looks and then looked back at Deante.

"Son," Detective LaFlore spoke after a few moments of Deante's crying, "Why don't you just start at the beginning."

Deante slowly lowered the tissue and looked at the detectives. "Hannah and I went to find firewood." Deante broke down again.

Detective LaFlore leaned back in his chair and brought his thumb and index finger up to the bridge of his nose. "All right, son. Why don't we start with you telling us about yourself? You play football, right?"

Deante cocked his head to the right. *How much information do they have?* "I used to. Not anymore."

Detective LaFlore cocked his head to the same side as Deante, mirroring him. "Used to? What happened?"

Deante sat up and exhaled. "I just," he paused, "got tired of it. Why does it matter? I thought you guys wanted to talk about the dead lady."

Detective Morris sat back in his chair. "Of course, we want to talk about that, but we wanted to understand you a little better."

"Is there a problem with that?" Detective LaFlore looked at Deante squarely.

Deante sat back in his chair and pushed his shirt sleeves up, exposing a tattoo of a cross on his forearm. "Nah, it's just that I'm tired and want to take care of this right away."

The two detectives nodded their heads in unison. "All right, son." Detective LaFlore picked up the reins again. "So, you guys decided to go and pick up some more firewood. And?"

Deante sighed in relief. "We were talking, and this nasty fragrance, I just – I wanted to identify what it was, and that's when we found the lady." Deante's phone began to ring. He pulled it out of his pocket and saw the word "Mom" on the screen. "My mom's here. I got to go."

The detectives nodded, and then one of them slid Deante his written statement. "Can you please sign off on your written statement?"

Deante grabbed the closest pen to him, didn't read the paper, signed it, slid it back to the detective, and exited the room, leaving both detectives in their chairs. After Deante left, the detectives looked at each other, grabbed the signed paper, and exited the room.

Deante was worried and relieved when he recognized his mother's car in the police parking lot. The engine was still running as he approached. After he heard the audible unlocking, he opened the door and climbed in.

Elyse sat in the driver's seat, staring at him. "Are you okay?"

"Yeah." Deante comprehended that the best thing to say was as little as possible.

"What did they ask you?"

"Just about how I found the lady."

"Did you sign anything?"

"Just my statement."

Deante slowly lowered the tissue and looked at the detectives. "Hannah and I went to find firewood." Deante broke down again.

Detective LaFlore leaned back in his chair and brought his thumb and index finger up to the bridge of his nose. "All right, son. Why don't we start with you telling us about yourself? You play football, right?"

Deante cocked his head to the right. *How much information do they have?* "I used to. Not anymore."

Detective LaFlore cocked his head to the same side as Deante, mirroring him. "Used to? What happened?"

Deante sat up and exhaled. "I just," he paused, "got tired of it. Why does it matter? I thought you guys wanted to talk about the dead lady."

Detective Morris sat back in his chair. "Of course, we want to talk about that, but we wanted to understand you a little better."

"Is there a problem with that?" Detective LaFlore looked at Deante squarely.

Deante sat back in his chair and pushed his shirt sleeves up, exposing a tattoo of a cross on his forearm. "Nah, it's just that I'm tired and want to take care of this right away."

The two detectives nodded their heads in unison. "All right, son." Detective LaFlore picked up the reins again. "So, you guys decided to go and pick up some more firewood. And?"

Deante sighed in relief. "We were talking, and this nasty fragrance, I just – I wanted to identify what it was, and that's when we found the lady." Deante's phone began to ring. He pulled it out of his pocket and saw the word "Mom" on the screen. "My mom's here. I got to go."

The detectives nodded, and then one of them slid Deante his written statement. "Can you please sign off on your written statement?"

Deante grabbed the closest pen to him, didn't read the paper, signed it, slid it back to the detective, and exited the room, leaving both detectives in their chairs. After Deante left, the detectives looked at each other, grabbed the signed paper, and exited the room.

Deante was worried and relieved when he recognized his mother's car in the police parking lot. The engine was still running as he approached. After he heard the audible unlocking, he opened the door and climbed in.

Elyse sat in the driver's seat, staring at him. "Are you okay?"

"Yeah." Deante comprehended that the best thing to say was as little as possible.

"What did they ask you?"

"Just about how I found the lady."

"Did you sign anything?"

"Just my statement."

Elyse's eyes widened. "Why would you do that? They could use that against you. How are you so stupid?"

Deante sat. He was annoyed, fatigued, and defeated. "Mom, I wrote it."

"So? Oh, dear Lord, help my son for being so stupid! Please, Lord." Her accent always seemed to get thicker when she prayed. "Lord, I need you to protect him from himself."

Deante rolled his eyes as she rocked in the driver's seat, praying zealously.

"Mom, can we please just go?"

Elyse cut her eyes at her son, shooting daggers at him as he interrupted her prayers. "How dare you. I'm interceding on your behalf, and you want me to stop and just – fine. We'll go, and if the police arrest you, then that's on you." Elyse threw the car in reverse, pulled out the parking spot, and started driving toward their home.

They sat in silence until Elyse started again. "I just try so hard. I did what I needed to raise you boys right, even after your father left me, and I had to pick up the pieces by myself. You stay in trouble, you realize that? From the football team to now. Then, when I try to help, all you do is talk to me horribly, just like your father. Sometimes, I wish I could just go to sleep and never wake up. If it wasn't such a horrible sin to kill myself, I would have done it a long time ago. But I don't want to go to hell. But sometimes you make me—"

"I'm sorry, Mom. Okay?" Deante had to stop her spiraling. Part of him wished he could have stayed in the police interrogation room. That would have been less pressure than being in the car with her. "I didn't mean it. But I read the statement. They didn't change anything. So, it's going to be okay," he lied. He had to say something to stop her from talking.

Elyse pulled into the driveway of their house. As the garage door rose, she opened her console and pulled out a bottle of anointing oil. Once the garage door was fully open, she pulled the car in, turned off the ignition, and turned to Deante. "Look at me."

He looked at her as she dabbed some of the oil on her index finger and made a cross on his forehead. She then grabbed his hand and prayed. "Lord Jesus, you said a disobedient child's life will be cut off, meaning that child will die. Lord, I ask that you make Deante accept that he needs to be obedient to me, or he will die. That's in your word. In your name, Amen."

"Amen." Deante jumped out of the car to get out of proximity to his mother. He grabbed his keys out of his pocket, unlocked the door, ran into the house, and into his room, where he shut and locked his door.

Safely inside his room behind closed doors, he finally slowed down and sat on his bed. He slipped his shoes off and put them in a neat line with his other pairs of shoes. Deante sighed, walked over to his dresser, and grabbed a tissue to wipe off the oil cross on his forehead when he caught a picture of him and his father leaning against the dresser mirror. Deante was flexing his muscles in his football jersey, with his father beaming next to him, wearing an ornate cross. It was the cross he always wore, the cross Deante ended up getting tattooed on his forearm.

Deante sighed, wiped the oil off his head, and threw the tissue in the overflowing trashcan beside his bed. He climbed into bed and stared at the ceiling.

Before Deante could reach for his phone or tablet, a loud series of knocks and the instant jiggle of his door handle invaded his small moment of peace.

"Deante," his mother's voice sailed through the door. "Come downstairs and help me make dinner."

"Yes, ma'am," he answered, but he stayed where he was for a few minutes until he got the strength to head downstairs and deal with more of his mother's abrasiveness.

CHAPTER 4

Lester pulled into the church parking lot, observing the sea of people clad in green and black. Taking a moment to check his appearance in the rearview mirror, he ensured his hair was neat and his green tie straight before stepping out of the car. Amidst the crowd, he searched for Gabi. His purpose there was to offer her emotional support. The multitude made it challenging to spot individual faces.

"Les! Lester!"

Turning, he caught her approaching in a white dress with a yellow belt.

"Les, what are you doing here?" Her accent became more apparent as she neared.

"Well," he contemplated revealing his true reason for being there, supporting Gabi in her grief over Lynette's death, but decided against it. "I never met the woman that died, but it just seemed right to pay my respects since she was part of the corporate family."

Elyse placed a gentle grip on his shoulder, her admiration evident. "That's amazing, young man. But let me tell you this," guiding him toward the church, she continued, "God makes no mistakes. If it was this woman's time to go, it just was. The Bible tells us that we all have to go, and the earth will spit our bones up like vomit, you get it?" She mimicked heaving, drawing confused and worried glances from those nearby. The attention embarrassed Lester. "So, she's gone, and there was no need for you to come here. You should be out enjoying your weekend."

Lester looked at Elyse inquiringly. "You don't think I should be here?"

Elyse gestured for him to sit on a bench, entering first and waiting for him. "No, in fact, I think this is all just a waste of time. We shouldn't spend time mourning the dead. They're already gone, and crying isn't going to bring them back. And for you to spend your time worrying about someone dead and gone is—"

Gabi walked past the pew they occupied. Lester swiped at her dress to get her attention. She nodded at Elyse and found a seat next to Parris.

Elyse leaned over to Lester, pointing in Gabi's direction. "She's someone who needs to worry about the afterlife, though."

Lester turned to Elyse, alarmed. "What do you mean?"

Elyse shook her head, eyes fixed on Gabi. "She's just so

arrogant. I tried to share the gospel with her, and she just spat it back in my face, saying she grasped everything I was saying. But if she did, she wouldn't be walking around, whoring herself at the company. She thinks she's smart, but what do I know. I'm just stupid compared to her. Stupid, stupid." Elyse began tapping her head aggressively, each repetition of the word "stupid" raising her voice. More people looked in their direction.

Unable to handle the attention, Lester grabbed an obituary from the pew in front of him featuring Lynette in a bed of clouds. Opening it, he discovered pictures of Lynette throughout her life, including a picture of her in her office, now his. A summary revealed she lived with her sister, now raising Lynette's two children, with a third child lost in the tragedy.

"She was pregnant?" Lester involuntarily spoke aloud, hoping the surrounding whispers would drown out his voice.

Elyse nodded. "Yes. They found out when they did the autopsy." Elyse perceived something, making her face go pale. She rushed to the back of the sanctuary, drawing more attention.

Deante entered the sanctuary, scanning for a seat in the back. Detectives LaFlore and Morris stared at him.

He approached them and shook their hands. "Hello, sirs."

"Hello, son." Detective LaFlore studied Deante's face. "What brings you here?"

Deante shrugged. "I mean, I found her. It just seemed right to pay my respects."

seemed right to pay my respects since she was part of the corporate family."

Elyse placed a gentle grip on his shoulder, her admiration evident. "That's amazing, young man. But let me tell you this," guiding him toward the church, she continued, "God makes no mistakes. If it was this woman's time to go, it just was. The Bible tells us that we all have to go, and the earth will spit our bones up like vomit, you get it?" She mimicked heaving, drawing confused and worried glances from those nearby. The attention embarrassed Lester. "So, she's gone, and there was no need for you to come here. You should be out enjoying your weekend."

Lester looked at Elyse inquiringly. "You don't think I should be here?"

Elyse gestured for him to sit on a bench, entering first and waiting for him. "No, in fact, I think this is all just a waste of time. We shouldn't spend time mourning the dead. They're already gone, and crying isn't going to bring them back. And for you to spend your time worrying about someone dead and gone is—"

Gabi walked past the pew they occupied. Lester swiped at her dress to get her attention. She nodded at Elyse and found a seat next to Parris.

Elyse leaned over to Lester, pointing in Gabi's direction. "She's someone who needs to worry about the afterlife, though."

Lester turned to Elyse, alarmed. "What do you mean?"

Elyse shook her head, eyes fixed on Gabi. "She's just so

arrogant. I tried to share the gospel with her, and she just spat it back in my face, saying she grasped everything I was saying. But if she did, she wouldn't be walking around, whoring herself at the company. She thinks she's smart, but what do I know. I'm just stupid compared to her. Stupid, stupid." Elyse began tapping her head aggressively, each repetition of the word "stupid" raising her voice. More people looked in their direction.

Unable to handle the attention, Lester grabbed an obituary from the pew in front of him featuring Lynette in a bed of clouds. Opening it, he discovered pictures of Lynette throughout her life, including a picture of her in her office, now his. A summary revealed she lived with her sister, now raising Lynette's two children, with a third child lost in the tragedy.

"She was pregnant?" Lester involuntarily spoke aloud, hoping the surrounding whispers would drown out his voice.

Elyse nodded. "Yes. They found out when they did the autopsy." Elyse perceived something, making her face go pale. She rushed to the back of the sanctuary, drawing more attention.

Deante entered the sanctuary, scanning for a seat in the back. Detectives LaFlore and Morris stared at him.

He approached them and shook their hands. "Hello, sirs."

"Hello, son." Detective LaFlore studied Deante's face. "What brings you here?"

Deante shrugged. "I mean, I found her. It just seemed right to pay my respects."

"That's nice of you, young man," Detective Morris said, patting Deante on the back.

Deante turned to find a seat. Seeing Elyse approaching, he immediately sensed trouble.

"What are you doing here? Who are these men?" Elyse's voice rose as she neared her son.

Worry evident on Deante's face, he searched for a good reason. "I just… I just felt bad for—"

"You were just being disobedient, like always. I swear to Jehovah I can't trust you to do anything I tell you to." She turned to the detectives. "And who are you, and why are you talking to my son?"

The detectives exchanged glances before responding. "Remember, Mrs. Semedo, we're investigating the homicide of Lynette Newble. We interviewed you when it was a missing person case." Detective Morris eyed her with concern.

"Correct, you did!" Elyse's voice rose. "What are you two doing talking to my son? He had nothing to do with this." She turned to Deante. "You, go home now. This is not a place for little boys. Do you understand me?"

Deante left the sanctuary.

Elyse returned to her seat next to Lester, leaving the detectives speechless. The funeral commenced as the organ played and the voices hushed.

Gabi picked up some empty plastic cups from the coffee table, rinsed them out, and placed them in her recycling bin. She smiled at Lester, who was gathering paper plates.

Since he sat with Elyse at the funeral, she avoided him. She didn't want to deal with Elyse and her foolishness. However, she texted a few coworkers, inviting them to her apartment afterward. Lester surprised her by coming and staying to help clean up.

After clearing the table, she swept the linoleum floors while Lester stared from the living room.

"How are you doing?" he asked.

Gabi focused on sweeping. "Guess what? I'm okay. It's been a struggle. To realize that at any time, you can be here, then gone. It just makes you face your mortality in a way I wasn't expecting."

Lester nodded slowly.

After sweeping, she grabbed her long-handled dustpan. "Then to know that not only did she leave two children behind, but she was pregnant too. What type of monster would do that to someone?"

Lester continued to nod, letting her vent without interruption. He didn't want to hinder the process.

"I'm very torn. You get it?"

"What are you torn about?" Lester asked, wanting to understand. Many things at the company were a mystery, and he needed clarification.

Gabi adjusted the trash bag and sat on the loveseat opposite Lester. She nudged her heel under the coffee table. "I socialized with Lynette at work, but she was a homebody. I'm trying to figure out why she was out so late, and the timing—"

"What timing?" Lester leaned forward, eager not to miss a word.

Gabi sat back, crossing her legs. "Okay, if I tell you something, can you promise it'll stay between us?"

Lester laughed. "I don't say anything to anyone, so go ahead."

"No," Gabi sat forward, uncrossing her legs, looking him in the eye. "I don't need this getting out to anyone, okay?"

"I promise. Everything stays with me," Lester assured, relaxing against the couch.

Gabi eased back, still deciding if she should share everything. "Alright, well, Lynette and Elyse had been feuding because of Elyse's son."

"The teenager she yelled at during the funeral?"

"No, but oh my goodness, wasn't that crazy?"

"Yeah, but go on," Lester waved it off, urging her to continue.

"Charles. That, 'Chuck for a Buck' or whatever that failure of a show is. That's Elyse's son."

Lester's eyes widened. "What? I had no idea."

Gabi nodded. "Yep. Lynette was messing around with Charles."

"Wait, I thought he was married. He had his wife and child on the show, in the commercial before, or something." Lester tried to remember.

"Oh yeah, he's married, but that didn't bother him while he was with Lynette. Rest in peace, Lynette." Gabi did a Catholic cross, kissed up to the sky, and continued. "Apparently, Elyse caught Lynette giving Charles head at his desk after hours."

Lester burst out laughing. "Oh, no! Not the moms walking in! That's like being in high school again."

Gabi laughed. "Yeah. Shortly after that, Lynette goes missing and then turns up murdered. No one else had information about the affair other than me, Lynette, Charles, and Elyse. To find out she was murdered, and later on, that she was pregnant? What are the odds? We're both old ladies. We don't stay past midnight." Gabi laughed at the thought. "It's all just conjecture. Who knows, but I don't trust Elyse and her too pious ass."

"Okay, I have to ask. What's the deal with you and Elyse?" Lester placed his arms around the back of the couch, getting more comfortable.

Gabi walked into the kitchen. "Would you like a drink?"

"What you got?"

"Water, soda, wine, and whiskey."

"Covering all the bases, huh?" Lester laughed.

"Sometimes I gotta take a few to the head after dealing with

Elyse. She's a real nutcase." Gabi laughed while she grabbed a chilled bottle of wine from her fridge and placed it on the counter.

"I'll take water."

Gabi grabbed a bottle of water and walked it over to Lester before heading back to the kitchen and pouring herself a glass of wine. "Okay, so everything was cool when I first started working there." Gabi walked over to the loveseat, sat across from Lester, and took a sip of wine before placing the glass tumbler on the coffee table. "She would stop by my office, and we'd talk for hours."

"How did you get any work done?" Lester wondered aloud.

Gabi shrugged. "I can chew gum and walk. I'm good at multitasking, so talking didn't stop me. It was the forced Bible studies."

"Did she drag you to Bible study?"

She rolled her eyes. "I wish. I'd be in my office working, and she'd be like, 'Look this scripture up on your phone.' I would do it, and then she'd be like, 'Read it.' So I would, but then she would stop me and make me repeat stuff."

"Like you were a child?" Lester had immediate flashbacks of going to church with his abuelita.

Gabi slammed her fists on the coffee table with each syllable. "Like. A Child!" She laughed and grabbed her glass of wine, taking a larger swallow than before. "My thing is, I don't mind listening to her talk about religion. I identify as a Christian, mind you. I'm not the best one, but I believe in Jesus and try to live in a way that if I had to express my actions to God, I can do so, and I'm willing to take the consequences. But she's not God, so for her to look down on me – child, please."

Lester laughed and took a sip from his water bottle.

"She always told me that if it was too much, to let her know, and we could stop talking about religion. Well, one day, I had a tight deadline, and she kept stopping me to read some scripture. The CFO kept sending his assistant to pick up the information, but Elyse waved her away. She told the assistant that what we were doing at the time was more important."

Gabi imitated Elyse's thick accent so flawlessly that it made Lester spit some of his water out. Gabi went to the kitchen, grabbed a paper towel, and gave it to Lester.

"When the assistant showed up a third time, I told Elyse maybe we should stop."

"She didn't like that, I bet," Lester said, getting up and taking the paper towel to the trash can.

"Hell, no, she didn't." Gabi and Lester both burst into laughter. "After that, she made my life a living hell. She would talk bad about me to the production manager, start all these rumors saying she caught me sleeping around the office when it was her son, not me, banging people on work property."

"Wow. So, what happened?"

"They had an internal investigation and identified how much she was lying. We had to talk to HR. Her foolish self admitted she didn't like me because she didn't like African American women."

Elyse. She's a real nutcase." Gabi laughed while she grabbed a chilled bottle of wine from her fridge and placed it on the counter.

"I'll take water."

Gabi grabbed a bottle of water and walked it over to Lester before heading back to the kitchen and pouring herself a glass of wine. "Okay, so everything was cool when I first started working there." Gabi walked over to the loveseat, sat across from Lester, and took a sip of wine before placing the glass tumbler on the coffee table. "She would stop by my office, and we'd talk for hours."

"How did you get any work done?" Lester wondered aloud.

Gabi shrugged. "I can chew gum and walk. I'm good at multi-tasking, so talking didn't stop me. It was the forced Bible studies."

"Did she drag you to Bible study?"

She rolled her eyes. "I wish. I'd be in my office working, and she'd be like, 'Look this scripture up on your phone.' I would do it, and then she'd be like, 'Read it.' So I would, but then she would stop me and make me repeat stuff."

"Like you were a child?" Lester had immediate flashbacks of going to church with his abuelita.

Gabi slammed her fists on the coffee table with each syllable. "Like. A Child!" She laughed and grabbed her glass of wine, taking a larger swallow than before. "My thing is, I don't mind listening to her talk about religion. I identify as a Christian, mind you. I'm not the best one, but I believe in Jesus and try to live in a way that if I had to express my actions to God, I can do so, and I'm willing to take the consequences. But she's not God, so for her to look down on me – child, please."

Lester laughed and took a sip from his water bottle.

"She always told me that if it was too much, to let her know, and we could stop talking about religion. Well, one day, I had a tight deadline, and she kept stopping me to read some scripture. The CFO kept sending his assistant to pick up the information, but Elyse waved her away. She told the assistant that what we were doing at the time was more important."

Gabi imitated Elyse's thick accent so flawlessly that it made Lester spit some of his water out. Gabi went to the kitchen, grabbed a paper towel, and gave it to Lester.

"When the assistant showed up a third time, I told Elyse maybe we should stop."

"She didn't like that, I bet," Lester said, getting up and taking the paper towel to the trash can.

"Hell, no, she didn't." Gabi and Lester both burst into laughter. "After that, she made my life a living hell. She would talk bad about me to the production manager, start all these rumors saying she caught me sleeping around the office when it was her son, not me, banging people on work property."

"Wow. So, what happened?"

"They had an internal investigation and identified how much she was lying. We had to talk to HR. Her foolish self admitted she didn't like me because she didn't like African American women."

"Wait, hold up!" Lester placed his water bottle on the table. "But she's an African American woman."

"No, she made it clear that she's an African woman living in America. She's not African American. Big difference."

Lester shook his head in disbelief. "So, she admitted this in front of HR?"

"Yep! With her dumb self. Then, when they told her that her remarks were grounds to fire her for discrimination, she tried to change it and was like: 'African American women just don't like me.' But I guess since her old, dried up, beef jerky looking butt has been there for decades they're just gonna let her work until she retires. Now we're not supposed to even speak to each other, which is why I turn all statue when I'm near her. I don't want to give her any type of ammunition to use against me. I could tell management that she keeps saying stuff about me, but I don't want to because then it would put her on the firing block, and I'm a freaking lady." Gabi laughed uproariously.

Lester continued listening in disbelief.

"The thing that gets me, though," Gabi grabbed her tumbler, admired it, and then took a sip. "For someone who claims to have such a high moral fiber, how dare she. Like seriously? That woman is pure evil. Then, she wants to talk about how her husband left her. Can you blame him? In fact, I wouldn't be surprised if she killed him. She didn't like how he prayed, so she just," Gabi pantomimed, putting a robe behind her neck and yanking at it. "That woman is just crazy. I can't wait for her to retire."

Gabi looked at Lester and found he was at a loss for words. "Oh, I'm sorry. I didn't mean to insult your best friend."

Lester laughed. "What do you mean?"

She placed her tumbler down and looked at him squarely. "Don't play dumb. It's not becoming of you."

Lester cocked his head. "Oh, so you got jokes?"

"Nah, I got truths. We both perceive her to like you. Probably because you're not an African American woman." Gabi imitated Elyse.

"Evil self. You probably shouldn't be here with me; you're with the enemy."

"What if I say I like living dangerously?" Lester smiled.

"You have to, based on the way we met." Gabi rolled her eyes and laughed. "It's just my luck that the guy I hook up with would be someone I end up working with."

"Not luck, synergy, maybe?" Lester laughed.

They continued to talk and laugh until Gabi walked him to the door.

CHAPTER 5

The hallways of Bridgeton High School were adorned with Halloween decorations as teens traversed, hurried, or rendezvoused opposite the lockers.

Over a month had passed since Hannah encountered the lifeless body in the woods, and with each passing day, the memory gradually faded. She was regaining a sense of normalcy and anticipated joining friends for her favorite holiday.

"Hey, boo!" Lisa sauntered up to Hannah, and the two embraced in their customary hug. "Ready to go to lunch?" A smile played on Hannah's lips, triggering a knowing look from Lisa. They always read each other like an open book.

Lisa recognized that closed-mouth, half-cocked smile as a precursor to some statement that might make her roll her eyes. "What? What kind of nonsense are you going to throw at me now?"

"I was thinking about meeting up with Deante in the library for lunch." Hannah expressed her plan, hoping Lisa wouldn't be too upset. Deante had been despondent after the incident in the woods, but he seemed to be coming around.

"Girl, do you, but—" Lisa groaned. "Look, I don't want you to think I don't want you happy. It's just—" Lisa peered at Hannah, sensing she was waiting for approval. Their bond was sisterly, and Lisa's opinion held great weight. "Have fun and be smart, okay? If anything happens, find me at the table, okay?"

Hannah's smile widened as she hugged Lisa. "Thanks for not being mad at me!" Hannah grabbed her book bag and headed to the study hall, but she stopped in her tracks. A chill ran down her spine as she became engulfed in a fog. Walking through the hallway was the woman she'd encountered in the woods. She discovered the gash on her forehead, the dirt-soiled clothes, the green shirt, and the leaves clinging to the fabric.

Lisa followed Hannah's alarmed gaze and saw the same figure. "For the love of God, Casey! Get the heck out of here!" Lisa shouted at the girl dressed as Lynette. The girl shrugged and nonchalantly exited through the nearest door. The hubbub of teenage voices persisted, unaffected by the scene. Everyone appeared oblivious to their surroundings.

Lisa scrutinized Hannah. "Are you okay?"

Hannah met Lisa's gaze, and gradually, color returned to her face. "Yeah, I just wasn't expecting to see that." Hannah took a deep exhale. "All right, I'm gonna go and meet up with Deante.

Wish me luck!" Hannah bounded down the hallway, ensuring to exit through a different door than Casey.

"Please be smart," Lisa murmured under her breath.

Lester sat in his car, waiting for Gabi to arrive after lunch. They had dinner at the Indian Palace, prudently choosing different arrival times to avoid any suspicions about their growing closeness. Despite this plan, Lester wanted to ensure Gabi's safe return to the studio.

Gabi pulled up in her sedan, immersed in dancing and singing to her radio.

Lester smiled, enjoying the sight of her grooving to the music until she passed the chorus.

Turning off the engine, she opened her car door, only realizing he was watching when he did the same, and their eyes locked. "Fool! You were supposed to be here before me! I'm wasting gas driving around the block, and you're just gonna walk in with me?" she teased.

"I told you; I like to live dangerously. And I had something for you." Lester leaned over and handed her a candied apple.

"Aww, sugar and fruit, my two favorite things." Gabi chuckled. They walked toward the building, laughing and talking, oblivious to Elyse standing near the entrance. As they approached, Elyse pushed the door open for them, her gaze fixed on them.

The smile on Gabi's face vanished as she muttered a quick "thanks" and walked in.

Lester felt a twinge of annoyance at himself but also a hint of relief that Elyse had witnessed them together. Elyse had been spending too much time in his office, and he hoped this would create some distance. However, he understood it was a delicate balance between what he needed to do and what he wanted.

"Thanks, Elyse."

"You celebrate Halloween?" Elyse eyed him distrustfully.

"Um, no. When I went to lunch, they were giving away free candied apples, so I decided to give it away instead of throwing it away," he lied.

"That's good because Halloween is the devil's holiday. Only evil people celebrate that day, so it was good for you to give the apple to Gabi."

Lester laughed awkwardly. *I can't believe she just said that out loud.*

"All right, so…" he wanted a quick exit to his office, but Elyse stepped in front of him, blocking his escape.

"I came because I wanted to invite you to the service my church has every Halloween. Please come." Elyse looked him squarely in the eye, almost daring him to decline.

"I'd love to come. What's the address?" *Irritated, but deciding to stay on Elyse's good side for now.*

Wish me luck!" Hannah bounded down the hallway, ensuring to exit through a different door than Casey.

"Please be smart," Lisa murmured under her breath.

Lester sat in his car, waiting for Gabi to arrive after lunch. They had dinner at the Indian Palace, prudently choosing different arrival times to avoid any suspicions about their growing closeness. Despite this plan, Lester wanted to ensure Gabi's safe return to the studio.

Gabi pulled up in her sedan, immersed in dancing and singing to her radio.

Lester smiled, enjoying the sight of her grooving to the music until she passed the chorus.

Turning off the engine, she opened her car door, only realizing he was watching when he did the same, and their eyes locked. "Fool! You were supposed to be here before me! I'm wasting gas driving around the block, and you're just gonna walk in with me?" she teased.

"I told you; I like to live dangerously. And I had something for you." Lester leaned over and handed her a candied apple.

"Aww, sugar and fruit, my two favorite things." Gabi chuckled. They walked toward the building, laughing and talking, oblivious to Elyse standing near the entrance. As they approached, Elyse pushed the door open for them, her gaze fixed on them.

The smile on Gabi's face vanished as she muttered a quick "thanks" and walked in.

Lester felt a twinge of annoyance at himself but also a hint of relief that Elyse had witnessed them together. Elyse had been spending too much time in his office, and he hoped this would create some distance. However, he understood it was a delicate balance between what he needed to do and what he wanted.

"Thanks, Elyse."

"You celebrate Halloween?" Elyse eyed him distrustfully.

"Um, no. When I went to lunch, they were giving away free candied apples, so I decided to give it away instead of throwing it away," he lied.

"That's good because Halloween is the devil's holiday. Only evil people celebrate that day, so it was good for you to give the apple to Gabi."

Lester laughed awkwardly. *I can't believe she just said that out loud.*

"All right, so…" he wanted a quick exit to his office, but Elyse stepped in front of him, blocking his escape.

"I came because I wanted to invite you to the service my church has every Halloween. Please come." Elyse looked him squarely in the eye, almost daring him to decline.

"I'd love to come. What's the address?" *Irritated, but deciding to stay on Elyse's good side for now.*

"No," her thick African accent made each word sound very staccato.

"Give me your address, and I'll pick you up."

"Sure. Can I text it to you?"

"Yes, just make sure you do it before you forget, okay?" Elyse looked at him.

"I'll text it right now." Lester pulled his phone out and texted his address. "Okay, sent it."

Elyse pulled her phone out and waited until she got his text. "Okay, got it. I'll see you at seven."

"See you then." Lester walked to his office and shut the door. Sitting at his desk, he began texting, "Lol, guess who's going to church tonight with your enemy?" Just before hitting send, he almost sent it to Elyse instead of Gabi. His heart dropped, then he erupted into a loud laugh. Shaking his head, he erased the message and placed his phone on his desk.

Hannah ascended the yellow and blue steps until she reached the library's double doors, her anticipation visible. Upon opening them, she scanned the area, searching for Deante. As she explored one wing and then another without spotting him, a worrying thought crossed her mind—did he stand her up?

"Hannah!" The relief washed over her as she spotted Deante

waving in her direction. He removed his headphones, peering at his laptop before pressing something on the screen.

Smiling, she walked over to him, placed her book bag down, and settled at the table opposite him. "Hey, so what are you doing up here?"

Deante shrugged. "My mother believes that Halloween is the devil's holiday. So, I've never participated in any of the activities to prevent hearing her mouth. I stay in the library, so I'm not influenced by any evil stuff, as my mom would say." Deante chuckled.

"Okay, so what are you doing on your computer?"

"Watching The Exorcist." He turned the laptop toward Hannah. The paused movie showed Reagan being put into the MRI machine to understand the cause of her bad behavior.

Hannah laughed, feeling at ease with Deante. Despite Lisa's opinion, she found him nice and polite. "So, what are your plans for tonight?"

Deante turned his laptop back to him. "Nothing. Usually, my mother makes me go to this church service about the dangers of Halloween, but she's been pissed at me, so I'm going to stay at home."

Now is your time, Hannah thought. Sporting the same half-closed, half-cocked smile she often gave Lisa when about to ask a favor, she said, "Well, no one should spend such an evil holiday alone. Want me to come over and hang out with you?"

Deante smiled. "Yeah, that'll be cool."

Loud talking erupted from the hallway, catching their attention. Deante's face turned ashen as he looked toward the disturbance.

Hannah turned and perceived Jared, a football player, walk in. Their eyes met, and he turned around and left.

"What was that about?" Hannah inquired, but Deante, already putting his headphones on, turned the movie back on. It was apparent he was in a sour mood. "Okay." Hannah hesitated before saying, "I guess I'll get with you tonight?"

Deante nodded, his jaw still clenched. "Okay, bye." Hannah walked away, more unsure of herself than ever.

The atmosphere in Lester's office was filled with a disappointed aura as Gabi sat across from him. "So, no scary movie marathon?" Her disappointment was evident in her expression.

"Nah, I gotta suffer at Elyse's church thing," he said with a smile.

Gabi managed to smile, but her annoyance couldn't be concealed.

"She ruins everything, doesn't she? You're gonna miss all of Frank's outdated quips and Parris' questions that make the movie seem longer to get through. All that for some church, huh?" Gabi sighed and stood up.

"It's cool, we'll miss you though."

"Scream for me," Lester teased.

"Oh, if you want me to scream, you gotta earn it," Gabi said. She walked to his door and found Elyse on the other side, looking through the window. Spotting Gabi, Elyse pivoted and walked away. Gabi turned and looked at Lester incredulously. "So you weren't going to tell me that that nutcase was burning a hole in my head all this time?"

Lester laughed. "I didn't see her. I promise."

"Yeah, go to church and pray for some better eyesight or something." Gabi shook her head and exited his office. She looked in the direction that Elyse walked down to make sure she wasn't still there.

"All clear," she whispered, laughing, and then shut his door.

CHAPTER 6

Detective Morris and Detective LaFlore escorted a tall, dark-skinned man into the interrogation room. Before entering, the tall man spat into a nearby trash can. Once seated, they all briefly regarded each other in silence before Detective LaFlore pressed record on the tape player.

"Today is October thirty-first, and this is Detective LaFlore with Detective Morris. We are about to talk to Charles Semedo. Now, Charles, just to let you know, you have the right to remain silent. Anything that you say can and will be used against you in a court of law. You have the right to have an attorney present. If you cannot afford to pay for an attorney, then one will be given to you. Do you understand your rights?"

Charles sighed and looked at the two detectives. "Yes, I understand."

"Okay," Detective Morris said, moving closer to the table. "Then let's proceed. Do you realize why you're here today?"

Charles looked around at both of them and then shook his head.

"No, why?"

"Well, why don't we start with Lynette," Detective LaFlore said.

"Who?"

Detective LaFlore looked at him, displeased. "Look, I understand that you spend your time putting it on for the cameras and an audience, but it won't work on us. Okay? Lynette Newble."

"What about her?" Charles' voice began to drip with annoyance as the conversation continued.

"Why don't you tell us about your relationship with her?" Detective Morris said, looking him in the eye.

"We worked at Oriflamme together. She was in Marketing. I have my own show, and that's it." Charles shrugged his shoulders, hoping they'd let him go soon.

"And that's it? You two just worked together, and…?" Detective LaFlore shrugged and shook his head.

"What else do you want me to say?"

"What about telling us about the affair?" Detective Morris said.

Charles rolled his eyes. "Why does it matter? Yeah, we had an intimate relationship, but it wasn't a big deal."

"How many times did you two engage in intimate activities?"

"I didn't count, maybe five or six times."

CHAPTER 6

Detective Morris and Detective LaFlore escorted a tall, dark-skinned man into the interrogation room. Before entering, the tall man spat into a nearby trash can. Once seated, they all briefly regarded each other in silence before Detective LaFlore pressed record on the tape player.

"Today is October thirty-first, and this is Detective LaFlore with Detective Morris. We are about to talk to Charles Semedo. Now, Charles, just to let you know, you have the right to remain silent. Anything that you say can and will be used against you in a court of law. You have the right to have an attorney present. If you cannot afford to pay for an attorney, then one will be given to you. Do you understand your rights?"

Charles sighed and looked at the two detectives. "Yes, I understand."

"Okay," Detective Morris said, moving closer to the table. "Then let's proceed. Do you realize why you're here today?"

Charles looked around at both of them and then shook his head.

"No, why?"

"Well, why don't we start with Lynette," Detective LaFlore said.

"Who?"

Detective LaFlore looked at him, displeased. "Look, I understand that you spend your time putting it on for the cameras and an audience, but it won't work on us. Okay? Lynette Newble."

"What about her?" Charles' voice began to drip with annoyance as the conversation continued.

"Why don't you tell us about your relationship with her?" Detective Morris said, looking him in the eye.

"We worked at Oriflamme together. She was in Marketing. I have my own show, and that's it." Charles shrugged his shoulders, hoping they'd let him go soon.

"And that's it? You two just worked together, and…?" Detective LaFlore shrugged and shook his head.

"What else do you want me to say?"

"What about telling us about the affair?" Detective Morris said.

Charles rolled his eyes. "Why does it matter? Yeah, we had an intimate relationship, but it wasn't a big deal."

"How many times did you two engage in intimate activities?"

"I didn't count, maybe five or six times."

"And that's all?" Detective LaFlore asked.

"Y'all, what's going on? Like, what do y'all want from me? I'm being honest, we were intimate a few times, and that was it."

"Did you hear she was pregnant?" Detective Morris asked, leaning on the table.

"No, I didn't know about that until it was released online. I don't even think she thought she was pregnant. But she was involved with other people too, so if you're looking for a motive, you have the wrong person."

Detective LaFlore smiled at Charles. "Well, since you have a motive, why don't we talk about an alibi?"

"I was at home. My wife can vouch for me."

"That's not really what we were talking about," Detective Morris said, leaning back in his chair. "See, we know you were home because your phone records place you there. Do you understand why that is?"

Charles stopped looking so confident as he gazed at them. "No, why?"

"Because we found Lynette's phone. Whoever took it probably attempted to discard it off a bridge, but it looks like they had pretty bad aim because the phone never reached the water. We looked through the phone, and you were the last person to talk to her."

"I don't remember that. Maybe I pocket-dialed her or something."

"Is that so?" Detective LaFlore asked.

"Okay, this is crazy?" Charles started looking around at each of them. "I want my attorney. I'm not about to get accused of something that I couldn't have possibly done because I was home."

"Not so sure of yourself now, are you?" Detective LaFlore said.

Charles cocked his head to the side. "Are you thinking that if you keep me here, you'll get some type of false confession out of me? I said I was no longer going to answer any questions, so anything I said after that cannot be used in court. So, I can confess if that's what you want. I can even confess that I stole the Lindbergh baby, but it doesn't matter anyway now, does it? So why don't you two open the door so I can go unless you want a civil lawsuit on your hands."

Detective LaFlore begrudgingly stopped the recorder. "You can go."

Charles got up and walked out of the door. Detective LaFlore and Morris exchanged knowing nods and also left the room.

Hannah smoothed her shirt down, got out of her car, and walked to Deante's front door. She was about to ring the doorbell when he opened the door, startling her.

"Hey," she said, embarrassed that she jumped.

Deante laughed. "Got the Halloween fright already, huh?" He moved over to the side to let Hannah inside.

Hannah had driven past Deante's house many times but didn't expect it to be so extravagant once she walked inside. To her right was a living room with all-white furniture. On the left was a dining room filled with mahogany fixtures. Walking further into the house, she peeped into a large room with twenty-foot-high ceilings and floor-to-ceiling windows. Everything looked extravagant, from the oversized couch that curved to the shape of the room to the matching chaise to the large entertainment center installed on the focal wall.

"Wow! Your house is so nice," Hannah said in awe.

"Thanks, my dad designed it."

Deante walked behind Hannah and hugged her.

Hannah had her reasons for being there and wanted just what he wanted, but she couldn't do anything until she got some answers.

She gently slipped away from Deante and turned around and faced him. "Hey, what was going on in the library today?"

Deante's face fell. He barely had the house to himself, and this wasn't something that he wanted to get into the first time he had a girl over. "I don't get what you mean." He tried to advance on Hannah again, but she stepped back and looked him squarely in the eye.

"You know what I mean. With Jared, in the library. I verified what happened. What's going on?"

Deante figured if he didn't tell her, she was never going to give him what he wanted. "Well, when I was on the football team, Jared and I got into a fight at a house party. It led to me being kicked off the team."

"What did you guys get in a fight over?"

Really? Deante was ready to let Hannah go home instead of talking, but when he looked into her face, he saw genuine concern.

Deante sighed. "He said something about my father leaving, and I just snapped. We were punching and pushing each other, and then," Deante tried to find a way to say this without scaring Hannah away, "we were fighting in the kitchen, and there was a knife on the counter. Jared reached for it first, but I was faster. I grabbed it and stabbed him."

"Wait, you stabbed Jared?" Hannah's eyes widened.

Deante couldn't tell if she was scared, but he regretted telling her the truth.

"Yeah, the police and ambulances were called. He was all right, but I got kicked off the team, and we're not supposed to be around each other." He looked back at Hannah, and her mouth hung open.

"So that's what happened? There were so many crazy rumors going around. And that makes so much sense because Jared had to take a few days off, and he was wearing that bandage. Oh, my goodness! I had no idea. That's so crazy," Hannah continued rambling.

Deante started moving toward the door.

"Where are you going?" Hannah asked, alarmed.

"I figured you wanted to leave, so I'm just unlocking the door for you."

"Nah, I'm cool," Hannah said confidently.

"Are you sure?"

Hannah nodded. "I promise. I'm sorry, I just wasn't expecting that story. I thought that maybe you two had the same girlfriend at one point in time or something. That's all. But I said I was going to hang out with you for Halloween, and that's what we're gonna do. So, do you want to watch movies in your room?"

Deante's eyes lit up. "Yeah." He walked to his room with Hannah following. *I'm so glad Mom cleaned my room for me*, he thought. He was annoyed when she was in his room earlier that day, but now that Hannah was gonna come in, he was grateful that she did. Once they got to his room, he shut the door.

Lester unlocked the door to his apartment, holding it open for Elyse. After a taxing twelve-hour day, fatigue weighed on him, but Elyse immediately requested to use his restroom before heading home. Lester gestured towards his bedroom, saying, "Just go into my bedroom, and it's to the left."

Elyse strutted into his bedroom, shut the door, and locked it. Lester, slightly offended by the invasion of his personal space, thought, *Okay, I wasn't going to go in my room while you're in my bathroom, but this is cool, too.*

Turning on the kitchen light, Lester grabbed a bottle of water from the fridge, taking a sip as he checked his phone for messages.

Gabi had texted: "I hope you had a great night! You were missed! See you tomorrow."

Smiling, Lester began to respond when Elyse flung his bedroom door open, brusquely walking out and startling him.

"Thank you so much for coming tonight, Les," she said, smiling.

No problem, he thought, adding internally, *Thank you for always giving me a freakin' heart attack, lady.* Aloud, he said, "Well, I think I'm gonna go to sleep."

Despite his social cues, Elyse approached him. "Can I just say how proud I am of you, Les?"

Surprised, Lester responded, "Why? I didn't do anything."

Elyse commended him, emphasizing his respectful and attentive nature. As she shared her experiences at Oriflamme, Lester experienced a chill, playing it off with gratitude, "Well, thank you, Elyse. I like to listen to people who are wiser than me and learn from them. So, thank you for taking the opportunity to teach me."

Elyse extended her hands for a hug.

Lester hesitated but decided to go along with it. As he went to hug her, Elyse tried to kiss him, prompting a quick pullback. "I'm sorry, Elyse, but I can't do that."

"Where are you going?" Hannah asked, alarmed.

"I figured you wanted to leave, so I'm just unlocking the door for you."

"Nah, I'm cool," Hannah said confidently.

"Are you sure?"

Hannah nodded. "I promise. I'm sorry, I just wasn't expecting that story. I thought that maybe you two had the same girlfriend at one point in time or something. That's all. But I said I was going to hang out with you for Halloween, and that's what we're gonna do. So, do you want to watch movies in your room?"

Deante's eyes lit up. "Yeah." He walked to his room with Hannah following. *I'm so glad Mom cleaned my room for me*, he thought. He was annoyed when she was in his room earlier that day, but now that Hannah was gonna come in, he was grateful that she did. Once they got to his room, he shut the door.

Lester unlocked the door to his apartment, holding it open for Elyse. After a taxing twelve-hour day, fatigue weighed on him, but Elyse immediately requested to use his restroom before heading home. Lester gestured towards his bedroom, saying, "Just go into my bedroom, and it's to the left."

Elyse strutted into his bedroom, shut the door, and locked it. Lester, slightly offended by the invasion of his personal space, thought, *Okay, I wasn't going to go in my room while you're in my bathroom, but this is cool, too.*

Turning on the kitchen light, Lester grabbed a bottle of water from the fridge, taking a sip as he checked his phone for messages.

Gabi had texted: "I hope you had a great night! You were missed! See you tomorrow."

Smiling, Lester began to respond when Elyse flung his bedroom door open, brusquely walking out and startling him.

"Thank you so much for coming tonight, Les," she said, smiling.

No problem, he thought, adding internally, *Thank you for always giving me a freakin' heart attack, lady.* Aloud, he said, "Well, I think I'm gonna go to sleep."

Despite his social cues, Elyse approached him. "Can I just say how proud I am of you, Les?"

Surprised, Lester responded, "Why? I didn't do anything."

Elyse commended him, emphasizing his respectful and attentive nature. As she shared her experiences at Oriflamme, Lester experienced a chill, playing it off with gratitude, "Well, thank you, Elyse. I like to listen to people who are wiser than me and learn from them. So, thank you for taking the opportunity to teach me."

Elyse extended her hands for a hug.

Lester hesitated but decided to go along with it. As he went to hug her, Elyse tried to kiss him, prompting a quick pullback. "I'm sorry, Elyse, but I can't do that."

Confused, Elyse offered a questionable explanation, "You misunderstand. See, I've been all over the world. I travel a lot, and that's how people say good night in Europe." Uncertain whether to accept her lie, Lester maintained an awkward silence until she apologized and left.

Following her to the door, Lester kept a respectful distance. She turned around, smiled, and said, "Thank you. Tonight meant a lot. You're like my son, and I appreciate it." Lester reciprocated the sentiment.

Once alone, Lester, filled with questions, grabbed his laptop, muttering as he checked his email for a crucial date. Discovering unsettling information about Lynette, he searched the internet for details, connecting the dots between her disappearance and his hiring. Panicking, he called Gabi, hoping for clarification.

The pieces fell into place for Lester as he realized the discrepancies in Lynette's departure. After a cryptic call to Kris, he secured his phone and settled in for a restless night, haunted by the revelations of the evening.

CHAPTER 7

Gabi and Lester met at the restaurant, enjoying each other's company. A sense of comfort enveloped Gabi when she was around him, and their conversation alleviated her loneliness.

Lester, too, seemed to find solace in their talks. As they sat in the cozy ambiance, Lester, genuinely interested, asked, "What's on your mind?"

Gabi sighed, her thoughts weighing heavily on her.

Lester admired her features—thick curly hair and smooth caramel skin. "I see that there's something on your mind. Go ahead, tell me."

Gabi readjusted, meeting his gaze. Her chest heaved as she began, "Here's the thing. I don't think you're being honest."

"What do you mean?" Lester inquired, frankly curious.

Gabi rolled her eyes, knowing he understood but needed to hear it. "I'm very open with you. I put myself out there. You perceive what I think and what I feel. Granted, it may be because I don't use my inner monologue like I should, but I've always been open and genuine with you. But I don't get the same from you. In my opinion, you're always holding back on something, and it bugs me."

Lester looked at her and shrugged. "I mean, I'm open with you. I took you to celebrate Dia de los Muertos with me."

Gabi shook her head. "Don't think I don't appreciate you inviting me into your life and culture; that's not it. The thing is," she sighed, considering her words thoughtfully. "Sometimes, it's like you'll get close to explaining something to me, and then you just stop. Almost as if you were censoring yourself. Like, you don't want to expose something. Or you'll ask me questions about things, and when I ask you what you need or want from me, you change the subject. Sometimes, my impression is that I'm being pumped for information, but I'm not sure why. It just doesn't feel like a safe environment, mentally, for me." Gabi looked up, debating whether to deny her next words but realizing it would be a lie. "I truly don't sense you are aware of this. It's as though you always get your questions answered, but I never get mine."

Lester nodded, understanding her perspective, but he couldn't reveal everything just yet. "You recognize how you can have a hunch about something, say it, and if it turns out that it's not true, then it's cool? Well, I can't. I've always been the type of person that I have to be knowledgeable before I can say anything. Before I can share any type of information, I want it to be correct."

"I understand, but it doesn't make me feel good that I'm helping you figure things out, and I'm all alone trying to understand things."

"I know," Lester acknowledged.

Silence settled between them. Gabi deserved answers, but Lester wasn't ready to provide them. Everything was still a hunch, and even if it wasn't, he couldn't disclose his thoughts or the limited information he had gathered.

"I guess we're at an impasse," Gabi said, smirking.

"I'm afraid so," Lester replied, seeing her face fall a little.

Gabi changed the subject, grabbing her menu. "What are you eating?"

Lester opened his menu and closed it. "A salmon salad."

"That sounds good."

The waitress came, took their orders, and left, leaving an unspoken tension lingering between them.

Lisa and Hannah strolled around the mall, each carrying a small selection of shopping bags. As they ascended the upward-bound escalator to reach the food court, Lisa asked, "Are you hungry?"

Hannah glanced towards the emerging food court. "Not really. I think I just want to sit. I hope we can find an empty table."

Upon reaching the landing, they discovered an empty table and settled themselves and their bags. Lisa, surveying the restaurants, remarked, "What's the point of dressing up for Thanksgiving? It's not like we're going anywhere. My mother will just complain that she's doing all the cooking, even if I attempt to help her, and then throw herself a pity party. We'll eat in misery; then I'll go upstairs and take a nap. A whole outfit for that foolishness?"

Hannah laughed, finding solace in the shared sentiment. "I viewed a meme, or something, where someone said we get dressed up on Thanksgiving, looking fresh as hell, and never go anywhere. I related to that on a spiritual level."

Lisa laughed and clapped her hands. "You know, like, can't we just sit in silence for the poor Indians who were murdered for this sham holiday?"

"Wrap ourselves in fake smallpox blankets?" suggested Hannah, and they both laughed.

"I guess I have more of a reason to dress up for Thanksgiving, seeing that Deante is going to come and meet my family." Hannah started doing a little dance in her seat while Lisa rolled her eyes.

"Well, I guess that is something to be thankful for. How is Stabby McStabster treating you?" Lisa inquired.

Hannah shushed her, looking around watchfully. "I told you not to tell anyone!"

"Fool, I'm talking to you." Lisa laughed.

"But still, don't say it so loud. I don't want him to think I'm telling all of his business." Hannah crouched down while speaking, trying to keep the conversation private.

Lisa shook her head and giggled, supportive of her friend's relationship but finding it ridiculous. "I'm going to grab a lemonade. You want something?"

"Umm… a water, please," Hannah said, straightening up.

"All right, I'll be back," Lisa said and headed toward the lemonade kiosk.

As Hannah looked around at the stores in the perimeter of the food court, she spotted a familiar clothing store. Now that she and Deante were dating, she was eager to buy some stylish clothing with a little sex appeal. However, her budget wouldn't allow her to shop at such a fancy spot.

"Hey, Ms. Bowers, how have you been?"

Hannah jumped, turning to see who was speaking to her. It was Detectives Morris and LaFlore.

"Sorry, I'm good," she said, looking at both of them and wondering if she was in trouble. "Um…how are you two?"

Detective Morris laughed, sensing her unease. "We're good. Just walking around, doing a little holiday shopping."

"We called your mom to check on you. She told us you were coming here. We just wanted to touch base with you," Detective LaFlore said, getting straight to the point.

"Touch base with me for what?" Hannah was confused, unsure how she might help them.

Detective Morris gestured to the empty seats, and Hannah signaled to Lisa, who was still in line. Once Lisa joined them, remarked, "What's the point of dressing up for Thanksgiving? It's not like we're going anywhere. My mother will just complain that she's doing all the cooking, even if I attempt to help her, and then throw herself a pity party. We'll eat in misery; then I'll go upstairs and take a nap. A whole outfit for that foolishness?"

Hannah laughed, finding solace in the shared sentiment. "I viewed a meme, or something, where someone said we get dressed up on Thanksgiving, looking fresh as hell, and never go anywhere. I related to that on a spiritual level."

Lisa laughed and clapped her hands. "You know, like, can't we just sit in silence for the poor Indians who were murdered for this sham holiday?"

"Wrap ourselves in fake smallpox blankets?" suggested Hannah, and they both laughed.

"I guess I have more of a reason to dress up for Thanksgiving, seeing that Deante is going to come and meet my family." Hannah started doing a little dance in her seat while Lisa rolled her eyes.

"Well, I guess that is something to be thankful for. How is Stabby McStabster treating you?" Lisa inquired.

Hannah shushed her, looking around watchfully. "I told you not to tell anyone!"

"Fool, I'm talking to you." Lisa laughed.

"But still, don't say it so loud. I don't want him to think I'm telling all of his business." Hannah crouched down while speaking, trying to keep the conversation private.

Lisa shook her head and giggled, supportive of her friend's relationship but finding it ridiculous. "I'm going to grab a lemonade. You want something?"

"Umm… a water, please," Hannah said, straightening up.

"All right, I'll be back," Lisa said and headed toward the lemonade kiosk.

As Hannah looked around at the stores in the perimeter of the food court, she spotted a familiar clothing store. Now that she and Deante were dating, she was eager to buy some stylish clothing with a little sex appeal. However, her budget wouldn't allow her to shop at such a fancy spot.

"Hey, Ms. Bowers, how have you been?"

Hannah jumped, turning to see who was speaking to her. It was Detectives Morris and LaFlore.

"Sorry, I'm good," she said, looking at both of them and wondering if she was in trouble. "Um…how are you two?"

Detective Morris laughed, sensing her unease. "We're good. Just walking around, doing a little holiday shopping."

"We called your mom to check on you. She told us you were coming here. We just wanted to touch base with you," Detective LaFlore said, getting straight to the point.

"Touch base with me for what?" Hannah was confused, unsure how she might help them.

Detective Morris gestured to the empty seats, and Hannah signaled to Lisa, who was still in line. Once Lisa joined them,

Detective Morris handed her his card and then passed one to Hannah. "Call us if you ever need to talk."

"Or if you find out any information, okay?" Detective LaFlore added. As the detectives walked away, Lisa sat down, worried about what had just transpired.

"What the hell was all of that?" Lisa asked.

Feeling overwhelmed, Hannah was relieved for Lisa's presence and ever-present cool demeanor. "I don't know," Hannah whispered, attempting to take a sip of her water but finding it difficult to hold anything down. A mix of fear, worry, and confusion overwhelmed her.

"Oh, my God, Hannah," Lisa whispered, pulling a few paper napkins from the dispenser on the table. "Do you want to leave?"

Hannah wiped her face, shook her head, and nodded when Lisa suggested sitting for a while. Confused, Lisa sat with her best friend, who silently cried. Although Lisa wanted to understand what was going on, she understood that now was not the right time to talk about it. She sipped her lemonade, waiting for Hannah to share.

CHAPTER 8

Lester stood on the sidelines, observing Charles host his weekly show, "An Hour on the Buck with Chuck." The show delved into financial planning, investing, getting out of debt, and effective ways to build credit. Today's episode revolved around family planning and recognizing one's limits when it comes to assisting others.

"I think we all would like to help others," Charles' baritone voice resonated through the open studio. "But I think we always need to know when we need to say no. If there's great risk in helping someone, and what I mean by that is if it's going to make your situation worse than what it already is, then it's okay to say no."

Lester nodded in agreement, well aware of the perils of giving more to others than he had for himself. After the funeral, when he and Gabi left the restaurant, she stopped talking to him. He understood it was a trust issue, but they weren't officially dating. They had met on an online dating app, and while he liked her, he still had a job to do. He couldn't share everything with her. So, he didn't pursue her, and she didn't pursue him.

The absence of their lunches and dinners left Lester more isolated. Even though their parting wasn't preceded by the typical lengthy conversations that often precede breakups, it was inevitable. They both expected things wouldn't improve if he couldn't change, and change wasn't imminent. It didn't stop him from missing her.

Gabi remained cordial when they crossed paths. If he joined the usual group at Burger Barn, she never made things awkward. It was as if their months of intimacy had been a dream, but when their eyes met, he internalized it was a reality.

Seeing her pass by the open studio door, Lester left and caught up with her. "Hey, Gabi."

She stopped and smiled while juggling a fistful of change. "Hey, Lester. What's going on?"

Walking with her, he shrugged. "Nothing much. I didn't have a lot of work today, so I decided to catch Charles' show."

"That's great. I need to grab some coffee. Sometimes, reading through all those contracts drains me." She headed into the break room.

Following her, Lester didn't know what he wanted to say, but he needed to say something. He wanted the emotional intimacy they had, to be with someone real and mature, not into playing games. He wanted to express all these thoughts, but instead, he asked, "Have you been watching Adult Swim?"

She smiled, walked over to the vending machine, and continued shaking the change in her hand while deciding what to get. "Yeah, but there've been so many reruns. I can't wait for the new season to come out."

Agreeing, Lester eyed her. "So, things have been cool?"

Gabi laughed as she approached the coffee pot, grabbed a disposable cup, and poured herself coffee. "I promise everything is fine." Grabbing a container of creamer, she asked, "Are you okay?" her tone suddenly serious.

He shrugged, "I guess I'm good. I miss talking to you, though."

Gabi grabbed a stirrer, poured creamer into her cup, and whisked it around. "Well, I am a very missable person," she teased.

As she walked toward the exit, she stopped and looked at him.

"I miss you too, but I can't give one hundred percent and only get seventy-five percent in return. But it's cool though."

Exiting the break room, she stopped when Elyse stepped in the doorway. Lester could imagine the stoic look on Gabi's face as she waited for Elyse to move.

Elyse seemed determined to stand her ground. "Well, Les, I'm not surprised to see Gabi being a loafer in here, but I didn't think you would be one too."

"Gabi wasn't being a loafer," Lester defended. "She was getting coffee to help her get more work completed."

Elyse looked at Lester with offense. "I just think it's funny that she decides to get coffee when you're in here." Her snide remark seemed harsher due to her accent.

Gabi didn't move. She was waiting for Elyse to step aside.

"I followed her in here," Lester said, growing irritated with Elyse's baseless rudeness.

Elyse looked dejected. Her shoulders slumped, and her gaze dropped to the floor, her features contorted into a sad expression. Evidently, she was no longer as confident as before, and her energy seemed to deflate as she moved aside to let Gabi pass.

Elyse approached Lester. "Look, I know you want to be noble and protect her, but you don't have to. Tell me the truth. Is she trying to waste time and be with you? If she is, she can get fired for stealing time."

Lester couldn't hold back his irritation. "Elyse, this is wrong. She did nothing. You're being rude and petty for no reason. I need to get back to work."

Lester left the room before Elyse could respond. He closed the door in his office, realizing his adrenaline was pumping. Sitting at his desk, he pulled out his cell phone and looked at Gabi's text message.

"Thank you for that," she texted.

He smiled and typed, "Anytime." He hit send and turned to his computer screen.

Hannah stood on Deante's doorstep. Chattering teeth and shaky hands betrayed her anxiety. The weight of unspoken words hung heavy, pressing on her as she grappled with what she needed to say.

Through the glass door, she caught sight of Deante's tall silhouette approaching. The door swung open, and he greeted her with a smile. "Hey, thanks for stopping by."

"Is your mom here?" Hannah inquired, her encounters with Mrs. Semedo in the past making her cautious. Despite an odd liking from Deante's mother, there was something off-putting that made her uneasy.

"Nah, she's working late today." Deante widened the door, inviting her in. "Are you okay?"

"No, I mean, I'm not certain. Have you been home all day?" Hannah asked, wringing her hands together, casting glances around to ensure Deante's mother wasn't lurking nearby.

"Yeah. I was just chilling." Deante's brows furrowed as he observed her pacing in the foyer. "Look, what's going on with you?"

"Did you get a phone call? If someone called your mother about you, would she tell you?" The urgency in Hannah's voice prompted Deante to intervene, placing his hands on her shoulders to halt her restless movements.

"Hold up. Stop. What the heck is going on?" Deante's concern was evident.

Bursting into tears, Hannah struggled to articulate, "Those

she decides to get coffee when you're in here." Her snide remark seemed harsher due to her accent.

Gabi didn't move. She was waiting for Elyse to step aside.

"I followed her in here," Lester said, growing irritated with Elyse's baseless rudeness.

Elyse looked dejected. Her shoulders slumped, and her gaze dropped to the floor, her features contorted into a sad expression. Evidently, she was no longer as confident as before, and her energy seemed to deflate as she moved aside to let Gabi pass.

Elyse approached Lester. "Look, I know you want to be noble and protect her, but you don't have to. Tell me the truth. Is she trying to waste time and be with you? If she is, she can get fired for stealing time."

Lester couldn't hold back his irritation. "Elyse, this is wrong. She did nothing. You're being rude and petty for no reason. I need to get back to work."

Lester left the room before Elyse could respond. He closed the door in his office, realizing his adrenaline was pumping. Sitting at his desk, he pulled out his cell phone and looked at Gabi's text message.

"Thank you for that," she texted.

He smiled and typed, "Anytime." He hit send and turned to his computer screen.

Hannah stood on Deante's doorstep. Chattering teeth and shaky hands betrayed her anxiety. The weight of unspoken words hung heavy, pressing on her as she grappled with what she needed to say.

Through the glass door, she caught sight of Deante's tall silhouette approaching. The door swung open, and he greeted her with a smile. "Hey, thanks for stopping by."

"Is your mom here?" Hannah inquired, her encounters with Mrs. Semedo in the past making her cautious. Despite an odd liking from Deante's mother, there was something off-putting that made her uneasy.

"Nah, she's working late today." Deante widened the door, inviting her in. "Are you okay?"

"No, I mean, I'm not certain. Have you been home all day?" Hannah asked, wringing her hands together, casting glances around to ensure Deante's mother wasn't lurking nearby.

"Yeah. I was just chilling." Deante's brows furrowed as he observed her pacing in the foyer. "Look, what's going on with you?"

"Did you get a phone call? If someone called your mother about you, would she tell you?" The urgency in Hannah's voice prompted Deante to intervene, placing his hands on her shoulders to halt her restless movements.

"Hold up. Stop. What the heck is going on?" Deante's concern was evident.

Bursting into tears, Hannah struggled to articulate, "Those

two detectives who talked to us after we found the body came up to me at the mall. They were just saying crazy stuff."

Deante stepped back, removing his hands. "Crazy stuff like what?"

"I don't know. It was—"

"What do you mean you don't know? You just came into my damn house talking about how the police said some stuff, and now you don't remember?" Is that what you're saying?" Deante's frustration escalated, catching Hannah off guard.

"I mean, yeah, I'm confused about what they said."

"Okay, what did they say then? Damn!" Deante demanded, his impatience palpable.

Hannah, now realizing her hands were vibrating with force, struggled to get the words out. "Um, they just said they were going to talk to you and that if I remembered anything to call them." She spoke slowly, afraid of saying the wrong thing.

Deante's exasperation was evident as his hands fell to his side. "That's it? That's all?" He scrutinized her for any signs of deception.

Terrified, Hannah nodded, tears streaming down her quivering chin.

A calm demeanor in Deante was replaced with growing rage. "You came over here to say that elementary mess? Sitting here crying and stuff? I thought you had something important to tell me. What's wrong with you?" His voice reverberated through the foyer.

"Deante, it wasn't what they said. It was what they didn't say. They made it seem like—"

"They made it seem like what? Because what it seems like is they were asking you normal questions, and your dramatic butt decided to make a big deal out of nothing."

"I'm sorry, Deante. It's just that they asked—" Hannah began to find her resolve.

"They asked nothing! You got me scared for a whole lot of bull!" Deante walked to the door and swung it open.

Hannah felt scared and useless, standing on the front step as if moving in a dream. From the food court to Deante yelling at her, none of it seemed real. But she realized it was all too real once the door closed behind her.

Deante paced impatiently in his room, grappling with uncertainty. The weight of the situation pressed on him, leaving him unsure of his next move. Should he call Hannah? Apologize? Acknowledge that she was right? The internal debate played out as he paced the confines of his room.

A fleeting thought of reaching out to his father crossed his mind, but the reality of a long-disconnected phone number and unknown whereabouts dampened the idea. Even if he could locate his father, would the man be of any help in this situation? The bitterness of abandonment surfaced. "Screw him. He left me; I don't need him," Deante mused, dismissing the idea.

Frustration mounting, Deante seized his cell phone and dialed his brother's number. As the phone rang, his conflicting emotions toward Charles surfaced.

"Hey," Charles's thick voice boomed through the phone.

Deante felt a mix of extreme relief and resentment toward his brother. "Hey, those detectives have been asking people questions about me."

"Don't worry, we got everything settled. You won't be bothered anymore."

"How can you say that? Do you know—"

"Dee," Charles interjected with an authoritative tone reminiscent of their mother. "Calm down, okay? I told you everything is okay. So be okay, okay?"

Deante, frustrated by Charles's lack of transparency, sat on the edge of his bed. "Okay."

As he opened his mouth to voice his concerns, his phone screen lit up, signaling the call had ended. Frustration boiled over, and Deante muttered, "Stupid ass," tossing the phone to the other side of the bed in frustration.

CHAPTER 9

The break room was abuzz with a sense of urgency as Lester entered. The usual calm atmosphere had been disrupted, with everyone engrossed in something on their phones or tablets. Sensing a change, Lester hesitantly spoke up, "Hey, y'all, uh… what's up?"

He was met with a synchronized pause as heads lifted up, akin to a group of zombies halting their pursuit. "Damn," Lester mumbled, contemplating a quick retreat.

Frank, however, approached him, holding out his phone. "Sorry, it's just, look at this." He handed the device to Lester, revealing an article from the Bridgeton Bugle featuring a sketch of an intricate Halloween mask.

"Okay, so?" Lester inquired.

"This is what Lynette's murderer wore," Frank stated.

Lester scanned the article: Months after the mysterious carjacking and murder of local woman Lynette Newble, police received a tip from an anonymous caller. The assailant donned this elaborate mask in the attack that took the lives of Lynette Newble and her unborn child.

"Wow." Lester looked up from the screen, meeting curious gazes from his colleagues. Gabi, in particular, seemed deeply engrossed in her phone. Concerned, Lester approached her and placed a hand on her shoulder. "Are you okay?"

She jerked away, a sharpness in her tone. "I'm fine," she retorted before snappishly leaving the break room.

"Whoa!" Lester was taken aback. Gabi's reaction was out of character, a departure from her usual even-keeled demeanor.

Frank attempted to explain, "Don't take it personally. She was close to Lynette. That's all."

But Lester sensed there was more beneath the surface. He followed Gabi's hurried steps down the hallway, witnessing her exit the office with keys in hand and a phone to her ear.

"Yes, I'll be there in like ten minutes," he overheard her say.

Lunch had passed, and Gabi remained absent. Lester's confusion and worry intensified. Something bothered Gabi, and it wasn't just the new tip on Lynette's murder. If anything, that revelation should have brought some relief, indicating progress in the investigation.

Concerned, Lester approached Parris in her office, seeking information. "Hey, where did Gabi go today?"

"I'm not sure. She just left and said she had something to do."

Parris peeked up from her computer to make eye contact with Lester.

Lester shoved his hands into his pockets. "Did she say she's coming back?"

Parris shook her head. "Nah, but I don't think she's coming back today."

"Really? Why do you think that?" Lester inquired.

Parris shrugged. "I called to get some forms I needed from her, and I was told she was gone for the rest of the day. They said she would be out of the office for the next few days."

Lester's mind raced with worry. "Okay, well…"

Before he could say more, Frank burst into the office. "You could try knocking!" Parris scolded.

"You could try shutting the hell up," Frank retorted. Turning to Lester, he delivered unexpected news, "The police are looking for you. They're in your office."

Lester recoiled in surprise. "Looking for me?" He hurried out of Parris's office.

"Can one of y'all shut my door?" Parris yelled, but Lester was already halfway down the hall toward his office.

Detectives Morris and LaFlore stood outside Lester's office, conducting a search. Lester approached them, puzzled. "I'm sorry, but what is this?"

The detectives exchanged smirks. "We received a tip that gave us reason to check your workplace."

received a tip from an anonymous caller. The assailant donned this elaborate mask in the attack that took the lives of Lynette Newble and her unborn child.

"Wow." Lester looked up from the screen, meeting curious gazes from his colleagues. Gabi, in particular, seemed deeply engrossed in her phone. Concerned, Lester approached her and placed a hand on her shoulder. "Are you okay?"

She jerked away, a sharpness in her tone. "I'm fine," she retorted before snappishly leaving the break room.

"Whoa!" Lester was taken aback. Gabi's reaction was out of character, a departure from her usual even-keeled demeanor.

Frank attempted to explain, "Don't take it personally. She was close to Lynette. That's all."

But Lester sensed there was more beneath the surface. He followed Gabi's hurried steps down the hallway, witnessing her exit the office with keys in hand and a phone to her ear.

"Yes, I'll be there in like ten minutes," he overheard her say.

Lunch had passed, and Gabi remained absent. Lester's confusion and worry intensified. Something bothered Gabi, and it wasn't just the new tip on Lynette's murder. If anything, that revelation should have brought some relief, indicating progress in the investigation.

Concerned, Lester approached Parris in her office, seeking information. "Hey, where did Gabi go today?"

"I'm not sure. She just left and said she had something to do."

Parris peeked up from her computer to make eye contact with Lester.

Lester shoved his hands into his pockets. "Did she say she's coming back?"

Parris shook her head. "Nah, but I don't think she's coming back today."

"Really? Why do you think that?" Lester inquired.

Parris shrugged. "I called to get some forms I needed from her, and I was told she was gone for the rest of the day. They said she would be out of the office for the next few days."

Lester's mind raced with worry. "Okay, well…"

Before he could say more, Frank burst into the office. "You could try knocking!" Parris scolded.

"You could try shutting the hell up," Frank retorted. Turning to Lester, he delivered unexpected news, "The police are looking for you. They're in your office."

Lester recoiled in surprise. "Looking for me?" He hurried out of Parris's office.

"Can one of y'all shut my door?" Parris yelled, but Lester was already halfway down the hall toward his office.

Detectives Morris and LaFlore stood outside Lester's office, conducting a search. Lester approached them, puzzled. "I'm sorry, but what is this?"

The detectives exchanged smirks. "We received a tip that gave us reason to check your workplace."

"A tip? Tip about what?" Lester pressed.

"Why don't we talk at the police station?"

"What? What's going on in this building?" Elyse, emerging from the crowd, questioned. "Why are you here again?"

"We're sorry to bother you, Ms. Semedo, but we have reason to believe that your employee might be connected to the disappearance and murder of Lynette Newble," Detective Morris explained.

"Wait, what?" Lester alarmedly interjected.

"Well, I'm not going to stop you from searching. If that will help clear his name, do so. But you won't find anything or receive knowledge," Elyse confidently declared, offering a reassuring smile to Lester.

"You won't find anything," Lester added, addressing the growing crowd of his coworkers.

"Dicks!" a voice from inside Lester's office yelled. People tried to file in, but Detective LaFlore blocked their way. An officer held up a gun, showing dried blood on it, placing it in an evidence bag.

"What's that?" Lester asked, bewildered. "That's not mine!" he pleaded, looking at Detectives LaFlore, Morris, and Elyse. "You guys, that's not mine!"

"What about this?" Detective Morris held up a bag containing a mask identical to the one sketched in the newspaper blog.

An audible gasp echoed through the room and the hallway, filled with what looked like almost every employee in the company.

"I've never seen that before in my life!" Lester protested.

"Really? Because your girlfriend discovered it under your bed, and we found it there," Detective Morris revealed, turning Lester around and handcuffing him.

Before Lester could say anything else, he was pushed out of his office into the hallway, all eyes of his coworkers fixed on him. There was a mixture of surprise, anger, and disgust as they eyeballed him being escorted out.

Detective LaFlore stayed behind. Spotting Elyse, he turned to her.

"Ma'am, have you noticed any weird behaviors with him lately?"

Elyse nodded emphatically. "Yes! I have."

"In that case, we need you to come to the station and give us a statement."

"Of course. I'll follow you guys there."

Lisa stood at the turnstile, directing families to purchase passes. The irritating children's songs blared over the loudspeaker, a constant reminder of her displeasure. Despite her disdain for the tunes, she found herself involuntarily bopping to the beat. After all, being bored and annoyed at work was preferable to the alternative of being broke and bored at home.

The door to "Jack's Rabbit Hole Burger and Pizza Emporium" swung open, and her heart sank as her blood boiled. Deante, accompanied by his pompous brother, the brother's wife, and their son, strolled in. The sheer disgust Lisa had for Deante at that moment surpassed the limitations of mere words.

Upon hearing Hannah's account of her last interaction with Deante, Lisa had to restrain herself from storming over to Deante's house and giving him a piece of her mind. While the desire to confront him still lingered, the need to keep her job and buy a Christmas outfit prevailed. She settled on a strategy of ignoring him while remaining cordial with his family.

"Hey, guys! Welcome to Jack Hole. Let me stamp your hands, okay?" Lisa dipped the stamper and rolled it gently on each of their right hands. When it came time to stamp Deante's hand, a fleeting desire to puncture or scratch him crossed her mind. Still, she restrained herself, wary of giving him any reason to retaliate. "Okay, you guys, have fun!"

As they walked past her through the turnstile, she let out an exhale of relief, silently thanking a higher power for preventing her from acting on her impulses. However, her moment of respite was short-lived.

"Umm, Lisa?"

The throbbing vein in Lisa's right eye betrayed her frustration. She refused to acknowledge him, keeping her back turned and pretending to be engrossed in the music.

"Lisa?" Deante stepped into her line of sight, making it impossible to continue ignoring him.

"What?" Her response dripped with venom, her response laden with disdain.

"Have you talked to Hannah?"

Deante thought it was a redundant question; Lisa and Hannah spoke every day. The absurdity of his inquiry was apparent, and Lisa's animosity towards him was palpable.

"What do you want, Deante?" Lisa shot back, hoping another family would walk through the door, providing an opportunity for him to take the hint and walk away.

"Look, I sense I was out of line with Hannah."

Lisa's head turned so swiftly that Deante worried it might snap off. "Out of line? Boy, are you serious right now?" Lisa glanced around, ensuring no one could overhear her impending verbal onslaught. She was willing to risk her job today. "You were an asshole. All she did was tell you that the police were asking about you, and you pretty much ripped her apart. But, baby, you got the right one now because I'll tell you everything that's wrong with your overrated ass."

Deante stood there, hoping Lisa could vent her frustrations so he could return to hanging out with his nephew. "Look, just say what you gotta say."

"Oh, I am! But let's get something straight right now, okay? No one asked you to come over here and talk to me. You brought your lanky, failed football career having self over here. Now, you've been poking at people, then want to get all crazy when they want to show their ass. But, baby, you gonna get this work, okay? Hannah is totally too good for you. You were lucky to even be allowed to breathe the same air that she did, and the fact that you had the gall to talk to her like that? You are a disgusting person. I hope nothing but bad things for you, and whatever the police were trying to find out about you, I hope it's all true."

"All right, Lisa." Deante finally walked away.

"Don't drop the soap, you punk," she shouted louder than she intended but didn't regret it.

Elyse sat in the interrogation room, her hands folded in front of her. The door was open, allowing her to detect other closed doors. She pondered the multitude of stories being told in those rooms, tapping her foot gently. Her mind wandered to Lester behind one of those doors, wondering about the lies he might be spinning to evade trouble.

Detectives LaFlore and Morris entered. "Thank you so much for coming to talk to us, Ms. Semedo," Detective Morris said, taking a seat opposite her.

"I want to be able to help," Elyse replied, smiling at them.

"That's great because we want you to tell us everything," Detective LaFlore added.

"Okay, well first, let me say, I expected Lester was trouble when he first came to the company."

"You did?" Detective Morris leaned forward.

Elyse nodded emphatically. "Oh, yes. He was late on his first day. I determined right then and there that he had no respect for people and their time."

"Really?"

"Oh yes. And there's something else. You see, God speaks to me. I'm a Christian. I don't just call myself a Christian. I go to church. I read my Bible. I go to Bible study. I do what God tells me to do, not what I want to do, but what God says, you know?"

Detective Morris nodded. "That's great. Having such a high moral fiber is great. It keeps people on the straight and narrow."

"Oh yes, it does," Elyse agreed. "See, I perceived that Les was bad and that he was going down a bad path. I tried to talk to him and warn him about the people that he was hanging around. Like that girl, Gabrielle." Elyse shook her head in disgust. "She's been nothing but trash. I would see her trying to seduce Lester. I tried to stop it. I invited him to church. Did he tell you that?"

"No, he didn't." Detective LaFlore sat back in his chair.

Elyse nodded even more. "He should have. I wanted him to be good. See, I know not everyone has just good or bad. It's a mixture. That's why we need Jesus in our lives. Without him, we would all be bad, doing bad things. But He," she pointed to the sky, shaking her head with reverence, "but He is the only good one. Do you mind if I pray? I just want God to help and bless you they want to show their ass. But, baby, you gonna get this work, okay? Hannah is totally too good for you. You were lucky to even be allowed to breathe the same air that she did, and the fact that you had the gall to talk to her like that? You are a disgusting person. I hope nothing but bad things for you, and whatever the police were trying to find out about you, I hope it's all true."

"All right, Lisa." Deante finally walked away.

"Don't drop the soap, you punk," she shouted louder than she intended but didn't regret it.

Elyse sat in the interrogation room, her hands folded in front of her. The door was open, allowing her to detect other closed doors. She pondered the multitude of stories being told in those rooms, tapping her foot gently. Her mind wandered to Lester behind one of those doors, wondering about the lies he might be spinning to evade trouble.

Detectives LaFlore and Morris entered. "Thank you so much for coming to talk to us, Ms. Semedo," Detective Morris said, taking a seat opposite her.

"I want to be able to help," Elyse replied, smiling at them.

"That's great because we want you to tell us everything," Detective LaFlore added.

"Okay, well first, let me say, I expected Lester was trouble when he first came to the company."

"You did?" Detective Morris leaned forward.

Elyse nodded emphatically. "Oh, yes. He was late on his first day. I determined right then and there that he had no respect for people and their time."

"Really?"

"Oh yes. And there's something else. You see, God speaks to me. I'm a Christian. I don't just call myself a Christian. I go to church. I read my Bible. I go to Bible study. I do what God tells me to do, not what I want to do, but what God says, you know?"

Detective Morris nodded. "That's great. Having such a high moral fiber is great. It keeps people on the straight and narrow."

"Oh yes, it does," Elyse agreed. "See, I perceived that Les was bad and that he was going down a bad path. I tried to talk to him and warn him about the people that he was hanging around. Like that girl, Gabrielle." Elyse shook her head in disgust. "She's been nothing but trash. I would see her trying to seduce Lester. I tried to stop it. I invited him to church. Did he tell you that?"

"No, he didn't." Detective LaFlore sat back in his chair.

Elyse nodded even more. "He should have. I wanted him to be good. See, I know not everyone has just good or bad. It's a mixture. That's why we need Jesus in our lives. Without him, we would all be bad, doing bad things. But He," she pointed to the sky, shaking her head with reverence, "but He is the only good one. Do you mind if I pray? I just want God to help and bless you guys on your way to convicting Lester. He's evil, and he needs to be behind bars."

Detective LaFlore and Detective Morris exchanged worried glances.

Detective Morris hesitated. "If you want to."

"Great, let's hold hands!" Elyse grabbed their hands, bowed her head, and started praying. "Dear Jehovah, Lord Jesus Christ, thank you for being here with us. You said that if two or more are gathered together, then You are in the midst. Thank you for helping us extinguish the evil that is in Lester. I pray that he will no longer lie. I pray that he will admit all the wrong he has done...in Jesus' name. Amen."

Elyse raised her head from the prayer, her face streaked with tears. Detective Morris pushed a box of tissues toward her. She wiped her face with one hand while raising the other in the sky, waving it from side to side.

"The Lord doesn't like it when we do bad things, so that's when you have to pray. Pray that the right people can get in trouble. Do you understand me?"

"Yes, we understand," Detective LaFlore said, rubbing his temple. "So, back to Lester. Was there anything he did in particular that made you suspicious?"

"Oh yes. See, he started off nice and sweet, and then when he started being around Gabi, he started acting evil with me. I remember one time we were in the break room, and he yelled at me because I asked Gabi what she was doing in the break room when she should have been working. He asked me why I was so concerned, and when I said his precious Gabi was stealing time and I could fire her, he started screaming at me. Like he was all in my face, and I was scared. I should have called the police then, but I prayed he would get his anger under control. I was scared for my life. I'm so glad you got him because if he could beat Lynette over the head with a gun, then God only knows what he could have done to me. Luckily for me, and because I know God, he protected me."

"That's true," Detective LaFlore said, exchanging a look with Detective Morris. "But let me ask you something. How do you know that Lynette was hit over the head with a gun?"

Elyse stopped for a second and replayed what she just said. "I didn't say that she was hit with a gun."

"Actually," Detective Morris said, "you did. Just now."

"Oh, well, I must have read about it in the newspaper. I read a lot. While most people are on their phones listening to horrible music, playing games, and watching dirty movies, I like to read. I read three chapters of the Bible every morning, and then I read the news, so I found out through that, that's all."

The two detectives exchanged looks and nodded. "It pays to be a good reader in this day and age," Detective Morris said.

"In fact," Elyse hit herself on the head as if she just remembered something. "When I first hired Lester, I was reading an article about what happened to Lynette, and when he scrutinized what it was, he looked at it, barely read it. It was as if he already had previous knowledge about what was going on. Then, he made some comments like, that's nice. I thought that was weird."

"That must have raised some red flags for you, huh?" Detective LaFlore said.

"Oh yes." Elyse began to rock in her chair. "I thought he's going to be trouble, but I wanted to be nice, the same way Jesus was nice to the lepers and whores. See, that's why, after all the evil things Gabi did to me, I treated her nice because God doesn't judge whores. He's just nice to them, and I want to be just like God."

"Okay, Ms. Semedo." Detective LaFlore put his hand over his mouth to stifle his laughter. He looked up at the camera in the corner of the room, knowing that this would make for a bizarre interview. He took a deep inhale to compose himself. "All right, so tell us about Lynette."

"Lynette was a hard worker. I wish she were still alive because she was great. She wasn't arrogant or angry. She just worked and went home. It was nice to have someone dependable and not going around being in people's faces."

Detective Morris adjusted himself in his chair. "Really? Because there were rumors that you two got into arguments pretty consistently."

"Oh no, not me." Elyse shook her head and started rocking in the chair. "I don't argue with anyone.

"There were also rumors that Lynette was having an affair with your son." Detective LaFlore said, inspecting Elyse's face.

"Please, I don't pay attention to rumors. And my son would never cheat on his wife. Do you know what I call rumors? I call them whispers in the dark because no one will say them in the light. See, Jesus operates in the light, but the devil works in the dark. I don't pay attention to what happens in the dark."

"But what if those rumors are true?" Detective LaFlore stated.

"Then I would say that you're wrong, Detective. I know my son. I know that he would never do something so evil. I raised my sons right. Now Deante, Deante might not do the right thing, but Charles always does."

"I have to let you know that when we questioned Charles a few months ago, we tested a sample of his saliva and DNA to that of the baby. Your son was indeed the father." Detective LaFlore reached into the inner pocket of his suit, pulled out the paternity results, and handed them to Elyse.

Elyse read them quickly, then handed them back. "That doesn't mean anything. DNA is fickle. They had DNA in the case of OJ Simpson, and he was able to get off. Just because they share the same DNA doesn't mean anything. We're all from Africa, so we're all related. And even if that was Charles' baby, that doesn't mean he murdered her. He was at home at that time. He told me," Elyse babbled.

"Did he also tell you that he was on the phone with her when she was attacked?" Detective LaFlore asked.

"No, and she probably called him. I don't think he would call her. Like I said, I know my son."

"Did he also tell you that he was texting someone at the same time that Lynette was attacked and that the number was pinging off of the towers around the area where her attack happened?"

Detective Morris watched Elyse as her face became ashen. She stopped babbling and looked at each of them, maintaining intense eye contact.

"Those things mean nothing. You have your murderer. You got him today. I viewed it all. He had the gun in his desk drawer, and you found the mask under his bed. So?"

"That's the thing, Elyse," Detective LaFlore said, smirking. "You always seem to know things before anyone else does. When the detective found the gun, it was out of the drawer when we came in. So, how did you know where it was?"

Elyse began to rock harder. She cocked her head to the side and held her eyes wide. She looked like a ventriloquist dummy vibrating with rage.

"For someone with such a high moral fiber, did you realize it's illegal to plant false evidence?"

"You're wrong!" Elyse yelled and slammed her hands on the table. "I would never do such a thing!"

"Oh, but you did, Ms. Semedo. And not only did you plant evidence, you planted evidence on an undercover police officer," Detective LaFlore said.

Just then, Lester opened the door and walked in, flashing his badge at Elyse.

"Elyse, you are under arrest for murder and obstructing justice. You have the right to remain silent." He read Elyse her Miranda Rights.

Elyse was in tears but said nothing.

Lester helped her stand up, placed her hands behind her back, and put her in handcuffs. He turned her around to face him. Her eyes were red but still wide, unblinking. They looked like cold glass marbles filled with hate. He thought for a second she was going to say something. Instead, she spit at him.

Detective LaFlore jumped up and led her out of the room.

"Thanks," Lester said to Detective LaFlore as he grabbed a tissue from the box on the table and wiped his face.

Detective Morris walked over to Lester and laughed. "How did you deal with that lady for all those months? I thought I was gonna bang my head through the table listening to her babble. I mean, Jesus Christ!"

Lester laughed and shook his head. "Hey, what room is Gabi in?"

"Two A."

"Thanks," Lester said quickly and left to find Gabi.

As Lester walked down the hallway, his mind buzzed with the surreal nature of the interrogation. He knew Elyse was involved

"No, and she probably called him. I don't think he would call her. Like I said, I know my son."

"Did he also tell you that he was texting someone at the same time that Lynette was attacked and that the number was pinging off of the towers around the area where her attack happened?"

Detective Morris watched Elyse as her face became ashen. She stopped babbling and looked at each of them, maintaining intense eye contact.

"Those things mean nothing. You have your murderer. You got him today. I viewed it all. He had the gun in his desk drawer, and you found the mask under his bed. So?"

"That's the thing, Elyse," Detective LaFlore said, smirking. "You always seem to know things before anyone else does. When the detective found the gun, it was out of the drawer when we came in. So, how did you know where it was?"

Elyse began to rock harder. She cocked her head to the side and held her eyes wide. She looked like a ventriloquist dummy vibrating with rage.

"For someone with such a high moral fiber, did you realize it's illegal to plant false evidence?"

"You're wrong!" Elyse yelled and slammed her hands on the table. "I would never do such a thing!"

"Oh, but you did, Ms. Semedo. And not only did you plant evidence, you planted evidence on an undercover police officer," Detective LaFlore said.

Just then, Lester opened the door and walked in, flashing his badge at Elyse.

"Elyse, you are under arrest for murder and obstructing justice. You have the right to remain silent." He read Elyse her Miranda Rights.

Elyse was in tears but said nothing.

Lester helped her stand up, placed her hands behind her back, and put her in handcuffs. He turned her around to face him. Her eyes were red but still wide, unblinking. They looked like cold glass marbles filled with hate. He thought for a second she was going to say something. Instead, she spit at him.

Detective LaFlore jumped up and led her out of the room.

"Thanks," Lester said to Detective LaFlore as he grabbed a tissue from the box on the table and wiped his face.

Detective Morris walked over to Lester and laughed. "How did you deal with that lady for all those months? I thought I was gonna bang my head through the table listening to her babble. I mean, Jesus Christ!"

Lester laughed and shook his head. "Hey, what room is Gabi in?"

"Two A."

"Thanks," Lester said quickly and left to find Gabi.

As Lester walked down the hallway, his mind buzzed with the surreal nature of the interrogation. He knew Elyse was involved in more than just being an overbearing mother. The revelation of her planting evidence added a new layer to the case.

He reached room 2A and gently knocked before entering. Gabi had her head on the table. She looked up as Lester walked in. Sitting up, tired and red-eyed, she fixed her gaze on him.

For the first time since knowing her, Lester couldn't read her expression, which scared him. Afraid she might say something that would sever their connection forever, he decided to dive in.

"I'm an undercover police officer. I was investigating Elyse. That's why I asked you questions and why I couldn't give you any answers. So, I guess I was using you, but I didn't mean to."

Gabi sat there, and her face fell. At that moment, she was devastated, and it showed.

Keep talking, Lester thought, not wanting that to be the last thing Gabi heard him say before she shut him out of her life. "We have reason to believe that Elyse's husband didn't leave her, that she murdered him."

Gabi stared at him. Her mouth dropped open in shock.

Lester nodded. *Okay, good. Keep talking,* he thought. "When I first started working there, I had no idea she was also behind Lynette's murder."

Gabi's eyes widened with that information.

"Wait, but what about the mask under your bed? I discovered it when I dropped my earring after using your bathroom." Gabi rubbed her temple, trying to make everything make sense.

"The night Elyse took me to her church, she used the bathroom in my room. She must have planted it under my bed then."

"See, don't you think it would have been better to just go to the scary movie marathon?" Gabi joked, smiling at Lester. The smile didn't have the same ease to it like it typically did, but Lester looked at it as progress.

"Since I was investigating her, it was better that I went with her to get her to trust me. I was hoping that she would have trusted me enough to reveal something incriminating, not try to set me up."

"So, I helped you catch Elyse?"

"Yes. You did a great job."

"That's it? I was there to help you," Gabi said. "I mean, I feel like I deserve some type of gift card, but everything we went through only amounted to her being behind bars?"

"No, Gabi," Lester shook his head. "You mean so much more to me than that. It's just that I couldn't tell you what was going on. I couldn't risk messing up the investigation."

"Did you ever really like me, or were you drawn to me because I was close to everyone and knew what was going on in the company?"

This time, Lester's face fell. He really liked her, but a part of him knew that if she wasn't as valuable with the information with the other coworkers, he probably wouldn't have spent as much time with her.

Tears began to fall down Gabi's face as she shook her head slowly. "You don't have to answer. I understand."

She stood up, grabbed her coat, and put it on. "I'm glad I was able to help, and I'm glad you were able to arrest her."

Lester continued to sit there. He put his head in his hands as he replayed the conversation in his head and tried to figure out if he could have fixed it. In the end, every time he thought of a different way he could have answered her questions, he knew that the ending would be the same.

Lester stood up and enveloped her in a comforting hug.

"Hey, it's over now," Lester whispered. "Elyse won't be causing any more trouble."

Gabi pulled away, wiping tears from her eyes. "I can't believe she was involved in all this. It's like a nightmare."

"I know, but we got through it. The truth came out." Lester paused, searching for the right words. "And about Lynette, justice will be done."

Gabi nodded, a mix of gratitude and sadness in her eyes. "Thank you, Lester. I'm sorry for thinking you killed her."

"I understand. But I couldn't say anything about the case. I hope you understand."

"I do now." Gabi smiled and reached out to give Lester one more hug. As they left the room, the hallway echoed with a mix of relief and tension. The case had taken a dark turn, but Lester was determined to see it through for Lynette, for Gabi, and for justice.

CHAPTER 10

Lisa struggled under the weight of three bags of trash as she made her way to the outdoor dumpster at the Jack Hole. The long shift had taken its toll, and all she wanted was to go home, especially to share her Deante encounter with Hannah.

A solitary light glowed on the dumpster, temporarily keeping the rats at bay. Once within tossing range, Lisa placed the bags on the ground and rotated her sore shoulders. Carrying those bags felt like an impromptu arm workout. When her arms finally ceased aching, she grabbed one bag and heaved it into the dumpster, repeating the act with the others.

Suddenly, a punch blindsided her, causing her to fall forward. Before she could process what happened, someone yanked her up by the back of her collar. Arms flailing, she struggled to comprehend the situation.

The assailant spun her around, and she found herself

face-to-face with Deante. In the glow of the singular light, his eyes appeared dark and soulless.

"What?" Lisa began, but before she could say more, he grabbed her neck, his grip tightening.

Lisa fought back, kicking and scratching. Desperation drove her to gather DNA evidence—scratching, clawing, and even inducing him to bite her. *Stupid fool*, she thought, slipping away as her surroundings blurred.

Lisa didn't want to die, but if she did, she was determined to leave behind a trove of evidence to convict him. Play dead, she coached herself, making her body limp while strengthening her neck, hoping it would be enough to make him release his grip.

Deante seemed unrelenting, refusing to let go of her neck, even as she feigned lifelessness. *This is it*, she thought, resigned to the idea of dying by a dumpster. As fatigue overcame her and she contemplated loosening her neck, she heard yelling.

"Hey! Hands up. Now!"

Released to the pavement, Lisa succumbed to a combination of blows and lack of oxygen, slipping into unconsciousness.

Coming to, Lisa found herself being loaded into an ambulance, an oxygen mask over her nose and mouth. Her neck, head, and back throbbed, each part of her body seemingly waiting for her to wake up just to flood her with pain.

Groaning, she attempted to shift into a more comfortable

position when an EMT intervened. "No, stay still. You're hurt, but you'll be okay, all right?"

For some reason, those words triggered tears. She was relieved to be alive but scared at how close she came to death. Facing her mortality, she harbored resentment towards Deante. She loathed herself for contemplating leaving her family and letting him win, but she was proud of ensuring he would be arrested for her murder. At that moment, exhausted but afraid to sleep, all Lisa could do was cry as the ambulance doors closed and the vehicle sped away with blaring sirens.

CHAPTER 11

Deante was handcuffed to the table, his face throbbing from the scratches inflicted by Lisa. This situation was unbelievable, a consequence of his anger spiraling out of control. Now, he was staring down the prospect of jail time for assaulting Lisa.

The door creaked open, and Detectives Morris and LaFlore walked in.

"Look," Deante began, "I wasn't going to kill her. I was just mad, okay. I just wanted to shut her up. I would have let her go."

Detective Morris raised his hand to silence him, pulling a recorder from his pocket and placing it on the table. Deante noticed another tape recorder already there. Confusion etched his face as Detective Morris pressed play.

Anticipating Lisa's raspy voice, Deante was confronted with his mother's unmistakable tones.

"It was all Deante's plan."

"What do you mean?" Detective Morris questioned.

His mother's voice continued, "When Deante found out that Lynette was pregnant by his brother, he went crazy. I tried to stop him. I told him it wasn't worth getting into trouble for, but you know him. He's crazy. I told you that he stabbed someone, right? When Deante is mad, he'll do whatever he wants to do."

Tears streamed down Deante's face as he listened to his mother's betrayal.

"So," Detective LaFlore interjected, "how did everything happen?"

"Well, Deante was hiding in the bushes by the movie theater, waiting for Lynette. He was supposed to hit her with the gun and scare her. I told him not to kill her, but I guess he did. See, that's what happens when you let the devil live in you. I would tell him all the time to go to church with me and be a good boy, but he wouldn't listen."

"And Charles had nothing to do with it?" Detective Morris inquired.

"No. See, Charles is a good boy. He would never do anything so evil. Yes, he did cheat, and the baby was his, but he would have never killed someone. That's all Deante."

The recording stopped, and both detectives stared at Deante as he buried his head on the cold steel table, overwhelmed with sobs. For years, he had harbored the fear that his mother might abandon him, and now, hearing the recording was a painful confirmation. She was throwing him under the bus, making it seem like everything was his fault when, in reality, he did it because his mother pleaded with him.

Deante's shoulders heaved with his sobs. He missed his father. His father had left him with someone as evil and hateful as his mother. Why would his father abandon him?

Detective Morris slid a box of tissues toward him.

"I'm so sorry. I'm so sorry," Deante repeated. "I wish my father was here." The words intensified his weeping. His heart was so broken, and the unloved, utterly alone pain was intensified. "But he left me too. I have no one."

Detective LaFlore leaned forward, looking at him. "Son, your father didn't leave you; he was murdered."

Deante looked up at both detectives, disgusted at the horrible insinuation. "Why would you say that?"

"Because it's true," Detective LaFlore stated. "She admitted murdering your father because he abused her."

Deante's mouth fell open. "She's lying. He never hit her!"

Detective Morris shrugged. "We can only tell you what she told us. She said that he hit her, and she'd had enough, so she killed him and buried him in the woods outside of the studio."

Deante shook his head. All this time, he thought his father had abandoned him when his mother had murdered him. Now, she had lied to the police, blaming Lynette's murder on him. Charles was involved, too.

Charles orchestrated Lynette's arrival near the movie theater, knowing she was pregnant, while Deante remained oblivious. Charles instructed Deante to dispose of the car and the gun.

Deante was his mother's pawn. He did whatever she and Charles told him to do. They wanted him to shoot Lynette, but fear gripped him, so he resorted to hitting her in the head again and again with the gun. Then, his mother encouraged him to pretend he stumbled upon Lynette's body, arguing it was inhumane for Lynette's family to think she was still alive when he killed her.

"Son, are you ready to tell us everything?" Detective LaFlore asked.

"What did my brother do?" Deante inquired, weighing his options.

"Your brother lawyered up," Detective Morris said. He didn't want Deante to follow suit, but he wanted him to know it was an option. Despite Detective Morris's sympathy for Deante, it paled in comparison to the grief he shared with Lynette's family. Her children were left without a mother.

"So, do you want to talk, or are you going to lawyer up too?" Detective Morris asked.

Deante looked at both detectives, exhausted. He couldn't lie anymore, especially after learning his mother had betrayed him. "I'll talk. I'll tell you everything you want to know."

Epilogue

"Hey, come on in here. We can't keep pausing the television for your fat butt!" Frank yelled from Gabi's living room.

Parris and Xavier laughed.

"Y'all are so close to getting kicked out of my place. I swear to God," Gabi said as she waddled over to the couch with her pregnant stomach bouncing.

"Are you sure you're done peeing?" Parris asked.

"Y'all are not about to pregnant shame me, okay? I can't help that my child is resting on my bladder. But if I pee on one of y'all, you're gonna play the victim," Gabi joked and lowered herself on the couch.

Xavier helped put her swollen feet up on the coffee table. "Your feet are looking like baked potatoes," he joked.

"Get out of my face." Gabi laughed. "Start this stupid show. Let's get this on and over with."

The title card, "Over the Edge," appeared on the screen.

"Ohh, fancy," Frank said.

"Shh," Parris said, as Nadene Watkins appeared on screen.

"It all started with a late-night drive. A woman running an errand in the small Midwestern town of Bridgeton. What seemed to be a distressing case of a carjacking gone wrong turned into a twisted tale of betrayal, deceit, faith, and murder, rivaling the craziest Hollywood scripts."

Next, Detective LaFlore appeared on screen.

"In the early hours of September twenty-second, Lynette Newble was driving and talking on her phone. The caller advised her to turn around in a movie theater parking lot after making a wrong turn. That's where she was assaulted."

A re-enactment showed a pregnant woman being pulled out of a car and beaten with the butt of a gun. Gabi, on instinct, rubbed her stomach as she watched the scene.

"But she wasn't found then, was she?" Nadene asked.

"No, it was three days later," LaFlore answered.

After LaFlore finished talking, Hannah appeared on camera.

"Every Friday night, some of the teens in the neighborhood would build a bonfire. This particular night, when we went to where we were going to build the bonfire, there was a weird, horrible smell. Most of us had second thoughts about building it after that. But it was Deante's first time, and he was looking forward to it, so even though it stank horribly, he talked us into having the bonfire. He said we needed more firewood, so Deante and I went to get some. That's when we stumbled on the body."

Everyone in the room began to frown and complain when

Elyse's picture appeared on the screen, and Hannah stopped talking.

"Just look at all that evilness on my television. I need to anoint it with oil after this is over." Gabi laughed.

"Or call a priest," Xavier said.

Lester appeared next. At that moment, everyone looked in Gabi's direction. "It's fine, you guys." She rolled her eyes and stared back at the screen.

"*Elyse Semedo reported her husband's disappearance three years prior. However, it was discovered that she had been giving away many of his prized possessions,*" Lester said, looking at Nadene. "*Elyse was known for babbling, for lack of a better word. She'd say things off-hand that made many people uncomfortable. She also made a few damning comments to other people. Some of those people contacted the police.*"

"*And that's when you got a job at Oriflamme Productions?*" asked the reporter.

"*Yes, it was an undercover operation to get close to Elyse and see if she would make incriminating statements again and see if she would reveal where he was buried. It was a little jarring when I ended up being the one to fill the position of the missing woman. I knew then I had to play it safe because who knew what Elyse was capable of?*" said Lester.

And we'll find out more when we return.

"Commercial break! All right, I don't know if I can handle all of this excitement," Frank said, laughing.

Gabi laughed as she struggled to get up. Parris rushed over to help her off the couch. "I've got to pee again. I'll be right back," Gabi announced.

"You got a ton of diapers for the baby. I don't know why you just didn't buy yourself some too." Frank yelled at her as she waddled to the bathroom.

Gabi entered her bathroom and quickly sat on the toilet to pee. When she was done, she grabbed some tissue to wipe but stopped. She could feel a tear threatening to fall, so she quickly dabbed at her eye and then exhaled. "You're okay, Gabi," she whispered to herself as she wiped.

She flushed quickly, washed her hands, and waddled back to the couch.

Nadene Watkins reappeared on camera as the show started again.

"Oriflamme wasn't just a production company. It was a place for family. But, it turned out to be a place of horror for people who went against the family. Like mobsters, anyone who crossed the Semedos had to be dealt with, even their own family members."

"Just watch; I bet all of the Godfather fanatics are going to start applying to work there now. If I have to work with them, I'm quitting. I'm telling you all now," Frank declared.

A picture of Charles Semedo sitting behind a desk for his show,

"An Hour On the Buck with Chuck," appeared and slowly disappeared to show a photo of an unhappy-looking Charles.

"Charles Semedo is Elyse Semedo's oldest son. We learned Charles not only had a knack for money-saving, he had a way with the ladies," Nadene announced.

"It was the worst kept secret at that company," Detective LaFlore said. *"I mean, he'd been caught with multiple women, but Lynette was the only one who he'd gotten pregnant and it probably angered him when she decided to keep the baby."*

"Do you think that's why she became a target?" Nadene asked, leaning forward.

"We know it was one of the reasons, but the other one we didn't see coming until Lester called us one night."

Lester looked at Nadene, waiting for her to prompt him.

"What did you find out?" Nadene asked Lester.

"I was hired three days after Lynette was pronounced missing. However, her position was posted as open while she was still working there. From all accounts, Lynette loved her job. She wasn't planning on leaving anytime soon, so for them to have her position open before she went missing sent chills up my spine."

"How did you handle that information?"

"I was assigned the same computer Lynette used. I did a search through her search history. That's when I stumbled across information about Elyse's husband."

The group in Gabi's living room noticeably gasped.

"I had no idea," Gabi whispered and then concentrated back on what Lester was saying.

"What we think happened was," Lester said, adjusting himself in the seat, "when Elyse was trying to bully Lynette to leave the company, Lynette did a little digging and found out that Elyse's husband had been missing a few days earlier than Elyse had claimed. Unfortunately, Lynette confided in Charles, not knowing he was in cahoots with Elyse. So, protecting each other, they got rid of Lynette, her evidence, and hoped it was the end of their problems."

Looking at the camera, Nadene said, "But that was just the beginning of their problems. Deante, in a flurry of hate, attacked a classmate and almost choked her to death."

Lisa was on camera next.

"He came to my job with his brother," Lisa stated. *"We got into an argument. I had to close that night. When I went outside, he was waiting for me. That's when he attacked me."*

"What went through your mind?" Nadene asked.

Lisa's eyes clouded for a second as she seemed to relive that moment. *"I decided that if he was going to kill me, I was going to get as much of his DNA on me as I could. So, I scratched him, hoping to get his skin under my fingernails, and then he bit me. I decided that if I was going to die, he was going to go down too."*

"And go down he did," said Nadene. "Police arrested Elyse

Semedo for planting false evidence in Lester's apartment and office. To get the heat off of her, she blamed it on her son, Deante.

"If you look at her interrogation, it was one of the most bizarre interrogations I've ever had in all of my career. She went through periods of praying, to yelling, to even spitting on Lester," Detective LaFlore said.

"It was despicable," Lester said, frowning, "but it was nothing less of what you'd expect from Elyse."

"And the courts got to experience the same weird behavior that the detectives did," Nadene announced.

There's a re-enactment of Elyse sitting at her table, rocking and looking at each person who testified and not blinking as they spoke.

"That actress got her down to a tee. That's exactly how Elyse was acting in the courtroom," Gabi said, still rubbing her pregnant stomach.

"There were so many outbursts that the judge threatened to muzzle her," Detective Morris said, shaking his head.

Nadene spoke up. *"But the biggest surprise came when Deante Semedo testified against his mother, Elyse Semedo."*

"Deante had already pled guilty, and we didn't offer him any type of deal," the prosecutor said, appearing on camera. *"He just wanted to get back at his mother for throwing him under the bus and also for murdering his father. Deante was very close to his father, and that seemed like a big motivation for him to get back at her."*

Deante appeared next on camera in his jail uniform. He was handcuffed, sitting across from Nadene.

"My mother manipulated me. She begged me to murder that woman, and then, when the heat was too much for her, she threw it at me. I'd had such a hard time dealing with what I'd done, and for her to be able to sleep placidly in it, I just couldn't stomach it anymore. There's no reason for anyone to take someone's life, but I feel like she felt okay with it because she didn't do it, but having someone else do something is just as bad."

"What Deante says is true," the prosecutor said. *"There's a saying that the hand of one is the hand of all. Meaning that if at any time someone is involved in the planning of an insidious deed, it's just as if they did the deed as well. Your fingerprints don't have to be on the gun if you goaded someone into pulling the trigger."*

"And how did it feel to face your mother in court?" Nadene asked.

Deante shook his head. *"It was hard. I mean, at the end of the day, that's my mother, but I knew that it had to be done. She'd done too much stuff and wasn't being held accountable, and I had to put an end to it. If I'm paying my dues, she has to pay hers."*

The camera panned on Nadene. *"And she did. Elyse Semedo was found guilty of first-degree murder, abuse of a corpse, planting false evidence, and hindering an investigation. She was sentenced to life in prison with 15 years tacked on for her other offense. Her son, Charles, was found guilty of accessory to first-degree murder and was sentenced to 25 years. Deante received 40 years."*

Semedo for planting false evidence in Lester's apartment and office. To get the heat off of her, she blamed it on her son, Deante.

"If you look at her interrogation, it was one of the most bizarre interrogations I've ever had in all of my career. She went through periods of praying, to yelling, to even spitting on Lester," Detective LaFlore said.

"It was despicable," Lester said, frowning, "but it was nothing less of what you'd expect from Elyse."

"And the courts got to experience the same weird behavior that the detectives did," Nadene announced.

There's a re-enactment of Elyse sitting at her table, rocking and looking at each person who testified and not blinking as they spoke.

"That actress got her down to a tee. That's exactly how Elyse was acting in the courtroom," Gabi said, still rubbing her pregnant stomach.

"There were so many outbursts that the judge threatened to muzzle her," Detective Morris said, shaking his head.

Nadene spoke up. *"But the biggest surprise came when Deante Semedo testified against his mother, Elyse Semedo."*

"Deante had already pled guilty, and we didn't offer him any type of deal," the prosecutor said, appearing on camera. *"He just wanted to get back at his mother for throwing him under the bus and also for murdering his father. Deante was very close to his father, and that seemed like a big motivation for him to get back at her."*

Deante appeared next on camera in his jail uniform. He was handcuffed, sitting across from Nadene.

"My mother manipulated me. She begged me to murder that woman, and then, when the heat was too much for her, she threw it at me. I'd had such a hard time dealing with what I'd done, and for her to be able to sleep placidly in it, I just couldn't stomach it anymore. There's no reason for anyone to take someone's life, but I feel like she felt okay with it because she didn't do it, but having someone else do something is just as bad."

"What Deante says is true," the prosecutor said. "There's a saying that the hand of one is the hand of all. Meaning that if at any time someone is involved in the planning of an insidious deed, it's just as if they did the deed as well. Your fingerprints don't have to be on the gun if you goaded someone into pulling the trigger."

"And how did it feel to face your mother in court?" Nadene asked.

Deante shook his head. "It was hard. I mean, at the end of the day, that's my mother, but I knew that it had to be done. She'd done too much stuff and wasn't being held accountable, and I had to put an end to it. If I'm paying my dues, she has to pay hers."

The camera panned on Nadene. "And she did. Elyse Semedo was found guilty of first-degree murder, abuse of a corpse, planting false evidence, and hindering an investigation. She was sentenced to life in prison with 15 years tacked on for her other offense. Her son, Charles, was found guilty of accessory to first-degree murder and was sentenced to 25 years. Deante received 40 years."

"When you think about how this turned out, it's just sad," Detective LaFlore said, looking at Nadene. *"You have a family that was so willing to protect themselves at all costs that they didn't mind destroying multiple people in the process. It was just collateral damage to them. That's scary when you think about it."*

The television screen went black as the credits scrolled.

"Oh wow, that was crazy. I can't believe we lived through all of that," Parris said, leaning back on the couch.

"Crazy, right?" Gabi said.

"Have you heard from Lester since?" Xavier asked Gabi.

Everyone looked at Gabi with bated breath.

"Nah. I mean, he sent me a congratulations text when my pregnancy announcement was posted in the Bugle, but that was it."

"I thought he was going to try to break up the wedding like DeWayne did at Whitley's wedding," Frank joked. "Baby, baby, please!"

"I...I do!" Gabi and Parris said at the same time, imitating Jasmine Guy's breathy voice in that scene. They all laughed together.

"Nah, I mean, Lester was an okay person, but I think it was understandable that he would never be able to give me what I needed. Also, how can I go back to someone who kinda used me?" Gabi said.

"But it was for the better good. If it wasn't for him, you would still be dealing with Elyse and her crazy eyes! Did you want that?" Frank exclaimed.

"No, but I shouldn't have to choose honesty and openness either." Gabi rubbed her stomach and played with her wedding ring. "Y'all, it's been three years since then, and I'm happy. My husband, Will, gives me everything I want and need. Every day, I'm confident that whenever he's talking to me, it's the truth. That means a lot."

"So, no regrets for not waiting for Lester?" Parris asked.

"Not a single one," Gabi said. "Not a single one," she whispered as she rubbed her stomach and smiled.

Book Club Questions

1. How did Gabi's personality and relationships influence the decisions she made? Did any specific relationships impact her journey the most?

2. Do you think Lester played with Gabi's heart?

3. In what ways does family loyalty play a role in the story? How does the matriarch's influence shape the choices of other family members?

4. How do Detectives Morris and LaFlore approach the case differently? What strengths do each of them bring to the investigation?

5. How are secrets presented in the novel, and what impact do they have on the characters and the community?

6. How does the town of Bridgeton contribute to the story's atmosphere? Would the story feel the same in a different setting?

7. What do you think about how conflicts were resolved? Were there any moments where you expected a different outcome?

8. The family matriarch goes to great lengths to protect her family. Do you agree with her actions, or do you think she crossed a line?

9. Were there any recurring symbols or themes in the story that stood out to you? How did they add depth to the plot?

10. Was there a moment or character that reminded you of a personal experience or a family dynamic? How did that affect your reading?

11. Were you satisfied with the ending? Do you think justice was truly served, or were there loose ends that left you wanting more?

Enjoy the first chapter of my fiction novel.

BROKEN SPIRIT

By Rose Jackson-Beavers

Chapter One

Bouncing and singing to the melodic grooves of Al Green, Stephanie was cheerful and in love. She knew every word to the song Al sang with perfection and confidence. She enjoyed singing the lyrics to "I'm Still in Love with You," her jam. Stephanie loved Al Green and listened to MAJIC 103 while singing her heart out. She popped her fingers and sang with her loud, alto voice vibrating throughout the car, putting her all into the song.

Excited about the prospect of seeing her man, Stephanie shimmied and danced to the song's beat. She missed Donnie and couldn't wait to see him.

Everyone considered Donnie Johnson a charmer. Stephanie met him two years ago at a charity affair for a mentoring program. He was a new manager, recently hired, at a local computer firm that had sent several of their managers to donate time and money to help the cause of keeping troubled teens out of jail by providing them with opportunities to work with professionals.

Donnie was a 32-year-old, six foot, bald-headed, caramel-colored brother who favored tailored suits and pressed, crisp, white shirts with neckties that blended well with his colors. He looked exquisite and reeked of money and good fortune. Plus, he had a mellow voice that transported unsuspecting females out of their underwear and into his bed without them realizing what happened.

After dating Stephanie for over a year, exclusively, he presented her with a flawless, white, four karats, square-cut diamond and asked her to marry him. She agreed. Now, their scheduled day to tie the knot was two weeks away.

As Stephanie turned into the Ridge Park subdivision, with its newly-built, two story, ranch-style, brick homes, the sound of her ringing phone interrupted her thoughts. She turned the music down and grabbed her cell off the passenger seat. She recognized the picture of her best friend's smiling face, as the name Regina and her number flashed on the screen. Stephanie smiled and pressed the answer button.

"Hey, girl." Regina's unmistakable voice filled her car. "What's up?"

The two friends met 20 years ago, at a Christian function. Regina Wilcox visited her church and they happened to sit together. They ended up chatting and exchanging phone numbers. The two girls were totally opposite of each other. While Stephanie flaunted a huge smile with perfect, white teeth and was considered by many as a beautiful, mocha-colored, brown-eyed girl with extremely long hair, who barely stood 5'4 in her clunky pumps, Regina was a gorgeous Caucasian, standing 5'6 and skinny with giraffe-like long legs that seemed to go on for miles.

The color of her hair served up a dark blond color, and her crystal blue eyes sparkled reminiscent of the sky. They reminded you of the clear, blue waters rolling up on the beach and cascading back into the ocean.

Both girls were beautiful. Stephanie's big ol' trusting heart seemingly got her in trouble. Always a friend to everyone, and even when someone hurt her, she would accept apologies and move on. Regina, on the other hand, was honest, critical of others, and held grudges. When they met, they were 11-years-old and just starting to wear clunky heels and the wrong color makeup and lipstick. But once they exchanged phone numbers, they became inseparable, even attending the same college and sharing rooms. These two ladies were thick as 20-year-old tree barks and stood together on issues even if the other wasn't too keen on the situation. They both came from upper middle class, educated parents and lived about 15 minutes away from each other.

The day they met, Regina's church visited Stephanie's congregation to participate in a concert as special guests. That was the beginning of an honest and beautiful relationship. Both girls dealt with their share of problems, bad boyfriends, and teary nights on the phone; but when things boiled down, they always counted on each other. While in college, Regina's family packed up and moved to Fort Meyers, Florida. But Regina accepted a job with a large, St. Louis firm as an attorney, which made Stephanie happy because she started her nonprofit company in the same area.

"Hey, Regina, girl, are you back in town?"

"Not yet. I'm still in Florida. I changed my plan due to a delay and won't return until next week sometime. My siblings want me to stay a little longer, since we haven't seen each other in a while." Regina pulled down her rearview mirror and wiped the excess lipstick from the corners of her mouth.

Turning her head to check out the homes in their new subdivision, Stephanie asked, "Well, how's your mom?"

"She's good, and she told me to tell you hi, and she'll contact you in two weeks." Smiling at her reflection in the mirror, Regina tilted the mirror up and focused on the road ahead of her.

"That's good. I cannot wait to see Mrs. Wilcox again. How many years has it been since I've seen her? Too many. I love your mom."

Frowning before responding, Regina stated, "Too bad Momma has to come to this wedding of yours to witness this travesty. I wish you would take my advice and not marry that fool."

"I still don't understand why you don't like him. He does so much good for the children and young men at the boys' club. He spends hours helping them with their homework and teaching them how to be good, young men."

"But, Stephanie, your problem is being blind. I'm concerned

by what you're not recognizing, and that bothers me. Remember that time you brought him to your company's party and he tried to talk to one of your friends?"

"He said he was playing." Stephanie rubbed the side of her face. The conversation was bothering her. She didn't want to remember the negative stuff.

Slapping her steering wheel in frustration, Regina asked, "What would you say if you were caught, red-handed, trying to talk to another woman?"

"Well, that happened then, and this is now. Donnie asked me to marry him and not anyone else. So, my dear best friend, although I love you dearly, please understand this is my decision and accept the situation."

"I am your best friend, which is why I have tried my darnedest to stop this. But, I'll leave your wedding alone. You, and only you, will have to live with your decision. I'll be here when you need me."

"That's all I ask, Regina. I just want you to support me. I'm happy, and that's all that should matter."

"I'll let you have this one, but the next time-"

"It won't be one, Regina, so let this go, please."

"I gotta go, girl, but I'll call you when I come to town next week. Be good; I love you."

"Love you too, girl. Smooches."

Stephanie pressed end call on her phone and sat the phone

back into the cradle on her car's dashboard. She smiled, thinking about the conversation. One thing she liked about Regina was her honesty.

Stephanie laughed as she drove through the subdivision. She lived in a beautiful area, but she and Donnie decided to sell their homes and purchase one together. They put their homes on the market and they would be on display throughout the month. They hoped someone would buy them quickly. Stephanie was ecstatic about a house she'd found and couldn't wait for her fiancé to view the structure.

She remembered the day clearly. "Donnie, let's check out this house in that new subdivision we passed the other day."

He reached over as he drove and squeezed her thigh. "If you let me bless you with some good loving when we arrive, I'll be happy to take a look."

"Boy, you silly if you think I'm going to lay on some filthy floor folks been walking over."

"You want me like I do you, right? I love you." He turned his head slightly to glance into her eyes.

"Boy, you better put your eyes back on the road." Stephanie took her two forefingers and pointed from her eyes to the street. "You better listen to me. Ain't nobody got time for car accidents."

"Girl, you feening for what I'm going to do to you?"

"I can't wait." Stephanie squeezed Donnie's right hand and

smiled. Happy and satisfied, things in her life were materializing the way she always dreamed they would.

Stephanie couldn't wait to sign the papers for the house they were going to buy together. About to visit Donnie's home, Stephanie drove up to the white, chain link fence with the multi-colored daisies peeking throughout multiple links. As she stepped out of her white BMW, she passed by the red, yellow, and pink flowers and leaned over to sniff the sweet fragrance lingering in the air. Stephanie stood up straight, tossed her thick, shoulder-length, auburn-colored hair back into the wind and strutted to the front door of the house to locate the man she would marry in two weeks. She used her key to open the front door. Stephanie was going to surprise her fiancé, who had no idea his lady had arrived home early from a business meeting in Los Angeles.

Stephanie was a day early, and she had missed him so much that she traded her seat for one on standby, just to arrive early enough to rush to the man who would soon become her life partner. She was excited because she had not seen him in five days. That's how long she counted since they had kissed or touched each other; she was excited to feel his loving arms wrapped around her waist as they became one.

Stephanie walked through the house with her white, 4-inch, crystal-covered sandals silently clicking on the beige carpet. She stopped and stood in the foyer, looking in the mirror to give herself a once-over before seeing him. Placing her Fendi, calfskin bag and car keys on the Balbo console table, she primped and turned to check out her appearance in the circular mirror. Her white, sheath dress that hugged her body emphasized her small waist and her sexy breasts that were deemed 'just right' by Donnie. Stephanie was gorgeous, but not conceited, and understood how to handle her looks. Although a sharp dresser, she focused more on her education and her work. Stephanie was grateful she didn't have a weight problem, but she was careful to present the right attitude of someone who was appreciative of life and charitable to others. Her parents had always taught her, in life, you attract more with sugar than salt. Her efforts to focus on her heart had always made her stand taller amongst her colleagues and others. She inspected herself in the mirror to ensure her appearance would be appreciated by her man who loved to flaunt beautiful women on his arm.

Pivoting, she walked toward the en-suite. She noted Donnie's Land Rover parked in the driveway when she pulled up to the fence. He was home. Since she had not bumped into him or detected any movement, she assumed he was in the bedroom. As she moved closer to their special spot, she heard their song blaring, which made her feel all joyful and unique inside.

It was their signature song, "The Point of it All," by singer, Anthony Hamilton. She practically jogged to the bedroom, thinking about what would be happening in 2.5 seconds. As she touched the doorknob, she heard something knocking up against the wall.

Twisting the doorknob, Stephanie nearly choked on the gum she was chewing.

"Oh, baby, your stuff is so good to me. Do your thing, girl." Donnie huffed and grunted out of breath.

"I love you." A woman, with her long legs wrapped around Donnie's back, screamed out as he pounded into her.

"Aww, baby. Don't stop." Donnie was thrusting himself into the woman, as if he had never experienced anything so good in his life. If Stephanie didn't know any better, she would think the man was crying.

The two, whipped fools sweet-talked and moaned so loudly over the music, they never even spotted her standing directly over their heads. Stephanie allowed the tears to pour from her eyes, as she searched the room for something to grab. The sting of betrayal begged her to kill Donnie. Not only that, he had mocked her by having sex with another woman while their song played in the background. Her heart pained with hurt and the feeling of rejection. She wanted to hurt him and make him experience the pangs of a broken heart like she was experiencing. Noticing the fireplace, she reached for the fireplace poker and walked in slow motion toward the man who had just crushed her heart. Lifting the poker up into the air, she slammed the deadly weapon across his head. Blood spurted out and spread quickly onto the screaming woman, who jumped out of bed and tried to run, but Stephanie was right behind her.

"Please don't hurt me. Please." The young lady looked no more than 20 years old. Her eyes bucked, and she looked like a deer blinded by headlights that was about to get hit by a speeding car. She looked terrified. Her straight, blond hair stood straight up on her head. Fear had caused her muscles to throb under her skin. Her pores began to exude sweat, and the hair on her arms, back, and neck started to stand up after seeing Stephanie swing the poker and strike Donnie with a violent blow to his head. The woman's entire body and brain were stimulated by fear. The young lady used her hands to hide her pale, white breasts, full, pink nipples and her private area, but her actions failed to cover her up. "I don't understand what's going on." She was inching toward the wall and reaching for her clothing. "Please, for God's sake, don't kill me. Who are you?" She cried. "Why are you doing this to us?"

"The question is, why are you in my fiancé's bed having sex with the man I am scheduled to marry in two weeks?"

Searching for her clothes, she stayed as far away from the crazed woman who was wielding a poker with a desperate look of anger and hate etched across her face. "This is my boyfriend." The lady screamed, as if she had been hit by a car. She slid her long, skinny, white body down the cream-painted wall; once on the floor, she scooted across the hickory hardwood to secure her dress that was bunched up in the corner. "Please don't beat me," she sobbed.

"You mean like you're doing me, slut?" Stephanie gripped the long, black, body of the poker and swung at the lamp on the table, which broke into tiny pieces while crashing to the ground.

The sound of the table lamp hitting the floor terrified the girl, and she pled for the stranger to let her go. "Please, lady, let me go. I don't know you, and I don't want to die."

"I'm not going to hurt you. But this two-timing fool over there, I am going to beat the mess out of him."

Pivoting around to focus on the one person she trusted, she tried to hold back her anger. A surge of hate and disgust so powerful consumed her body and thoughts that she believed she would die from the energy in the room. She rushed to the bed where Donnie lay bleeding to finish him off. Stephanie raised the poker and Donnie's eyes fluttered open. He jerked to full attention and rolled off the bed. As he tried to stand up, he staggered like a drunkard leaving a bar.

"Are you crazy, Steph?" He shook his head to gather his senses. Donnie asked and grabbed a towel off the chair next to the bed, pressing down on his head to halt the bleeding. He walked toward Stephanie with his other hand raised. "Please, baby, this means nothing."

Seeing his private member dangling made her madder. With her left hand, she covered her left ear, as if she was trying to block out the noise. She was about to hit him again when she caught a voice saying: Don't do this; it's not worth jail. Stephanie. Put the poker down and flee.

"No." She screamed, as she swung the poker up into the air,

missing Donnie. But before she brought the poker down again, the voice interrupted, Flee, Stephanie; now.

Dropping the poker, she turned and sprinted to the front of the house, grabbed her purse and keys off the table, opened the door, ran to the car, and jumped inside. She made it safely and locked the door as Donnie, who was running behind her, almost on her heels, took a brick and tried to break her window. He was screaming like a person suffering from behavioral issues, as he chased the car, naked, with the towel still pressed against his head.

The car was speeding out of control as Stephanie pressed the accelerator as hard as she could. She looked out of her rearview mirror and realized Donnie had stopped and wrapped the towel he used to wipe the blood from his head wound around his waist as a small crowd started to gather.

Stephanie was despondent. All she could think about was killing herself. She could not believe this was happening to her. She thought she had found the one - the man of her dreams. She thought she could trust him, but like all the rest, he was a liar and a lust-filled idiot. He didn't wear a condom. How many times had he exposed her to diseases?

Kill yourself, an obnoxious-sounding voice barked. Don't nobody want you. You keep getting hurt. Life isn't worth it.

She hit the steering wheel so hard she injured her hand, which only made her cry harder as she tried to shake away the pain. "Please, God, please help me."

Other Books by Rose Jackson-Beavers

Fiction

A Sinner's Cry

Broken Spirit (Returning characters from A Sinner's Cry)

Mental Health

Breaking Behavioral Health Barriers in Faith-Based Communities

Bottled Up Inside: African American Teens and Depression

Christian Devotion

Journey to Jesus with Me

Teens

A Hole in My Heart (Part 1)

A Holiday Wish (Part 2)

Caught in the Net of Deception

All other books can be found on Amazon, Barnes and Noble and anywhere books are sold.

www.ingramcontent.com/pod-product-compliance
Lightning Source LLC
Chambersburg PA
CBHW022345271224
19560CB00037B/1002